C000093296

GOLD ON THE HOOF

VOLUME 3 OF THE AMES ARCHIVES

PETER GRANT

SEDGEFIELD PRESS

Copyright © 2019 by Peter Grant. All rights reserved.

Cover image cropped from *A Dash for the Timber*
by Frederic Sackrider Remington
Cover design by Beaulistic Book Services

This book or parts thereof may not be reproduced in any form, stored in a
retrieval system, or transmitted in any form by any means – electronic,
mechanical, photocopy, recording, or otherwise – without prior written
permission of the author and publisher, except as provided by copyright law in
the United States of America.

This is a work of fiction. Names, characters, places, and incidents are products
of the author's imagination or are used in a fictitious manner. Any similarity to
actual people, organizations, and/or events is purely coincidental.

This book is dedicated to my wife, Dorothy.
She's my strong right arm,
and I rely on her support every day.
Thanks, darling.

CONTENTS

1

The hands gathered around the corral, exchanging quiet remarks as Jeb, the stablehand, saddled the big black bronc. The horse snorted and quivered, clearly wanting to rend limb from limb the puny human who dared to put so alien a burden on his back. However, he was securely held by the rope around his neck, pulling him tight against the snubbing post, and the blindfold over his eyes prevented him from seeing his tormentors.

"You say he hurt Jaime real bad?" Walt asked as he studied the big mustang.

"*Si, señor,*" Vicente, the leader of the band of *mesteñeros,* replied softly. "That horse is the toughest we've ever caught. I know our agreement is that we bring you only horses we have three-saddled, but this one... I thought about shooting him after he threw Jaime so hard, but then I realized you might want him as a stud stallion. His offspring can be tamed young and early, before they become too much like him. He is all heart, and determined to be free; but he is also a killer. Even so, I have seldom seen a horse this good."

"He's not bad-looking, for sure. Still, Nate wants to wring him out. He reckons he can ride any horse ever foaled, so we'll see if he's right."

"You do not wish to try him yourself, *señor?*"

Walt held up the steel hook on his left wrist. "Before this, I would have, but with only one hand, that'd be taking a foolish risk."

Vicente sighed. "I had not thought of that. You are right, *señor* Ames."

Nate Barger, Walt's ranch manager, strode up to the corral and stepped through the bars. Crossing to the horse, he checked the bridle, reins and saddle cinch, then said, "All right, he's ready. Leave the blindfold on, hobble him, and lead him to the dam."

The small crowd of onlookers followed as the big black stallion was led out of the gate by a rider. He did not struggle, having learned the futility of fighting a rope around his neck.

Bringing up the rear, Walt said to Vicente, "You only brought a dozen horses. I'd expected a lot more."

"*Señor,* I am sorry to say it, but the herds of mustangs are not what they once were. Even worse, that is our fault – people like me."

"Huh? Seems to me there's still plenty of wild horses out there."

"Yes, *señor,* but their quality is much poorer. For years, *mesteñeros* such as I have driven herds of wild horses into capture chutes, picked out the best to three-saddle and sell, then driven the culls out again. It would have been better for the rest of the mustangs if we had shot them. All the time we were taking the good breeding stock out of the herds, while the culls went on breeding more like themselves. Now, there are few really good mustangs left. Most are spavined, narrow-chested, cow-hocked, knock-kneed, pigeon-toed... all the things no buyer will accept. Where I used to capture two hundred or more good horses each trip, ten years ago, now I am lucky to find twenty to thirty. That means I must charge more for them if I wish to make a living, but few buyers will pay higher prices, because there are so many cheap cow ponies coming up from Texas. For buyers like you, who want quality stock, it is different; but few of the animals I capture today will meet your standards. I was lucky to find twelve for you."

Walt rubbed his chin thoughtfully. "When you put it like that, it makes sense. What'll you do when it's no longer worth going after the mustangs at all?"

Vicente shrugged. "That time is very near. I shall try to make a living breeding better-quality horses, but it will be difficult, and I will not be able to keep all my men. Some of them may become *vaqueros* – what you call cowhands – or transport riders."

"Waal, as it happens, I may be able to help you there. Talk to me tomorrow morning. I may have work for you and some of your men through the winter."

Vicente nodded, a smile appearing on his face. "I shall, *señor*."

The dam was a fold of land some distance to the right of the buildings. It had been widened and deepened by convict labor during the summer. Walt had found that the prisoners, usually despised and distrusted by potential employers, had worked amazingly well after being assured that, for every week the work went well, he'd provide a full-on barbecue for them on Saturday night, with plenty of meat and all the trimmings. He'd also promised to pay each of them a bonus when the job was completed, instead of just paying the prison its labor rate. The dual incentives had persuaded them to work hard for him. The dirt they dug out had been used to construct a retaining wall, and a layer of clay had been laid in the dam bed. An irrigation pipe led from a stream in the hills, two miles away, to the rear of the dam, to keep it filled. An extension from the pipe led to a rail-road-style water tower that supplied the compound's buildings, leaving the dam water for irrigation and for animals.

The onlookers gathered on the shore as Nate and the stablehand removed the hobbles, then led the stallion into the water. It snorted and trembled as it was led deeper, until the water was halfway up its body, covering the saddle's stirrups. Nate waited until the rope had been removed, then clambered into the saddle, took up the reins, and settled himself. The horse quivered with fury as it felt the hated man-presence on its back; but, still blind-folded, it could do nothing but wait until it could see once more.

"All right, Jeb. Pull off the blindfold and get the hell out of the way!"

"Yessir!"

There was an explosion of spray as the big stallion, vision suddenly regained, erupted into a series of high, straight bucking jumps, trying to dislodge the rider from its back. Jeb dived clear and half-ran, half-swam to the bank, where he was hauled out of the water by his friends. They watched in awe as the black crow-hopped, sunfished, and twisted its body in half-moons to left and right.

Nate held on for dear life. The depth of the water prevented the horse from using its full strength and agility, so he was able to stay astride for a couple of minutes. However, the black managed to edge closer and closer to the bank, until its body was clear of the water. Suddenly it launched a high, straight buck, and wrenched its haunches hard to one side at the peak. Nate was thrown clear in a soaring arc, splashing into deeper water and disappearing beneath the surface. The black whirled and tried to run clear of the dam, but was instantly lassoed by a waiting, mounted wrangler. Trembling, snorting, it halted just clear of the shallows, and stood still, panting and puffing with exertion.

Nate surfaced, blowing water from his mouth and snorting, grinning broadly. "*Yaaa-hooo!* That's a fightin' hoss, I'll tell a man! Blindfold him again, and lead him back into deeper water."

He was swiftly obeyed. He climbed back into the saddle, and the fight recommenced. The big horse crawfished, crowhopped, wormed and spun, but Nate held it in deeper water where its strength could not be fully exerted. For almost ten minutes it threw itself in all directions, but could not gain enough momentum to eject its rider from the saddle.

At last it slowed, then stopped moving, standing still in the water, sides heaving. Nate slid from the saddle, standing chest-deep in the water, and moved slowly to the horse's head, speaking in a soft, soothing tone, stroking its mane, then its nose. The animal clearly wasn't happy with being touched like that, but it was too exhausted to do anything about it. Nate gentled it for a few moments, blowing lightly into its nostrils.

At last he signaled to Jeb. "Put the blindfold back on, then lead him back to the paddock. Let him dry out in the sun, and make sure he's got fresh hay and water. Put the saddle out to dry, too. We'll do that again tomorrow morning. After a few days in the dam, he should have calmed down enough that we can try him on dry land."

"Yessir! What're you gonna name him?"

"That ain't my call. Ask the boss."

The stablehand turned to Walt. "Boss?"

"I don't know yet, Jeb. I don't even know if I'm going to buy him. Let me think on it."

"Aw, come on, boss! You gotta buy this one! He's too good to let go!"

"Not if his temper's so bad that he takes it out on a rider, or a stablehand. How'd you like him rearing up and hammering those hooves into your head?"

Jeb flinched visibly. "I guess I wouldn't like that at all."

"Neither would we. Let's see if Nate can break him to the saddle. That'll help. Meanwhile, you move *real* careful around him, you hear? Make sure you've always got a way to get clear if he goes wild on you. Never let him pin you where there's no way of escape, like a closed stall."

"Yes, *sir!* I'm gonna treat him like he was made o' pure dynamite, with a blasting cap in each hoof!"

Nate laughed. "Yeah – and one up his ass!"

Laughing, the small crowd broke up, turning to head back to the ranch buildings.

2

As they walked past the barns, Walt peered towards a rider approaching the main gate. His face broke into a grin. "If that ain't Jim Dunnett, I'll eat my hat! Vicente, see to your other horses. I'll dicker with you about them tomorrow morning. I've got to greet this man."

"*Si, señor.*"

By the time the new arrival reached the gates, Walt and Nate had made it down to the administration building. Walt waved and called, "Hi, Jim! Must be almost half a year since we last saw each other."

The rider rode up and dismounted, grinning, offering his hand, which Walt shook firmly. "About that, I reckon."

"This long drink o' water here is Nate Barger. He's one of those who helped me take down Parsons and his men. He stayed on to be my manager here on the horse ranch. Nate, this is Jim Dunnett, the Colorado Ranger who helped us find Parsons."

"Howdy, Mr. Barger." The two men shook hands.

"Nate, please. I've heard a lot about you from Walt. I'm sure not more than half of it was true, though!" They chuckled.

"Knowin' him, it was less than half of a half! You're all wet. What happened?"

"Been breakin' a new horse to the saddle, up at the dam. They can't use all their strength in deep water – it slows 'em down. I reckon I'd better get some dry clothes on." Nate nodded to Walt, then headed for his quarters.

The visitor sniffed appreciatively, looking across at the fire pits where two whole oxen were turning on spits over coals. "Them beeves sure do smell good! What're you celebratin'?"

"We've got men arriving today. We started barbecuing two oxen yesterday evening. They should be ready by suppertime. You're just in time to help eat 'em." Walt indicated the grinning boys who were turning the carcasses on spits over beds of coals, basting them frequently with sauce. "Their sisters are helping their mommas get the rest of the food ready in the cookhouse." He gestured to the central building behind them, which was bustling with activity.

"You've built a nice place here," Dunnett observed. "Got a bed for me tonight?"

"For you, anytime. You can join Nate and I in the headquarters building. We have guest rooms. What brings you out here?"

"You do. I've been hard at work tyin' up all the loose ends you handed us over the Parsons affair. Turned out to be a whole lot more complicated than anyone expected. You did me a helluva favor when you brought back all that evidence and gave it to me."

"I did?"

"Yeah. First off, after sortin' through all the title deeds, bearer share companies an' other papers, the Territory's recovered more than a quarter of a million dollars through sellin' off all Parsons' stolen property."

Walt whistled. "That's a whole lot more than I figured." This horse ranch had been established on another of Parson's former properties, more than sixteen square miles of the Wet Mountain Valley, after Dunnett had given his blessing. Since Walt had spent upwards of twenty thousand dollars of his own money to get Parsons, the Ranger had reckoned he'd earned it as compensation. "Did they let you keep any of the money?"

"*Ha!* No chance o' that! It did me a power o' good in another way, though." Dunnett glanced at Walt. "Remember that big ledger you gave me, with details of everyone Parsons had bribed or blackmailed for information?"

"Yeah. I reckoned it oughta come in useful."

"It sure did. Thing is, after what happened to the first batch o' papers you handed over, I figured it'd be smart to keep the ledger safe." Both men frowned at the memory of how Parsons had used his political connections to shut down Dunnett's initial investigation, and confiscate and destroy the evidence Walt had provided. "I had the ledger copied, and handed in the copy, keepin' the original. I got it here in my saddlebags for you."

"And did anyone try to interfere with it?"

"Oh, hell, yeah! I had politicians crawling out o' the woodwork, running scared in all directions. I wasn't allowed t' file charges against 'em, although some clerks an' bureaucrats got busted. Thing is, they knew they couldn't just make the ledger 'disappear'. I ended up havin' a private interview with someone important, who I ain't allowed to name. He told me straight up that he couldn't act against everyone I'd identified, 'cause it would cripple the Territorial government. It might even affect our chances o' becomin' a state soon. Even so, he said he was sorry he couldn't turn me loose on 'em. We made a deal. I gave him enough to seize an' auction off the rest o' Parsons' properties. He saw to it that all the money went into the Territory's account, rather than get stolen all over again. I double-checked, to make sure he did."

"An' what did he give you?" Walt asked.

Dunnett grinned, and flipped back his vest to expose the badge pinned to his shirt over his left chest. Last year, it had been a star within a shield, labeled simply 'Colorado Ranger'. It was now a six-pointed silver star, with the words 'Deputy' and 'U.S. Marshal' inscribed, respectively, above and below central text reading 'Colorado Territory'.

"You're a U.S. Marshal now?" Walt exclaimed. "How'd you fix that, movin' from Territorial to Federal law?"

"The man I talked to sent me to see the Territorial U.S. Attorney. He got real interested. Told me the federal government's plannin' to go after corrupt Territorial officials across the West, an' the evidence you an' I got between us might help 'em do it. Don't talk about that to anyone else – not yet, anyway." Walt nodded. "Y'see, the federal gummint can do things that'd be political suicide for a territorial Governor, an' that's just what they're fixin' to do. Upshot was, I resigned as a Ranger, an' took both copies of the ledger with me. I started work as a Deputy U.S. Marshal the very next day. Got a nice pay raise, too, which didn't hurt none. Gave my new boss the copy of the ledger, and brought the original back here to you."

"Why me? I can't do anything useful with it."

"Not right now, maybe, but by killing Parsons and busting up his criminal network, you exposed a lot of politicians an' businessmen who ain't got any reason to like you. They may make things difficult for you in future. If anyone does, look up his name in Parsons' ledger, and see what you find. If he's mentioned there, he might back off if you tell him about it."

Walt grinned. "If you weren't such an honest lawman, I'd reckon you'd been taking lessons from Parsons' ghost about how to handle politicians! I'll be sure to do that. Come on. Let's put your horse in the stables, then I'll take you to the guest room."

Jim led his horse after Walt, looking around with interest. The ranch buildings formed a deep U shape. At the base was the big central building, housing the cookhouse, dining hall, living quarters for the kitchen staff, and general storerooms. A big bathhouse, with a lean-to structure containing a boiler, occupied one end. To the left stood a long bunkhouse, able to accommodate up to fifty men, divided into four sections. It was matched on the other side of the U by an equally long building containing the ranch offices, residential apartments for Walt and Nate, an armory, and several more storerooms. Three big horse barns stood behind the U, each with a hay barn attached, and a blacksmith's forge and leatherworker's shop beside them. Corrals stood on either side, with sheds, open at the sides, protecting wagons, horse-drawn mowers, and several large stacks of firewood against the elements. Worker's cottages had been erected nearby, and tents were pitched in a row beyond them.

"This is turning into a big operation," Jim said seriously as he handed over his horse, then followed Walt to the administration building. "I hadn't expected you to be this far along."

"I decided to do most of the setup work first," Walt explained as he led him inside. "I hired workmen in Pueblo in the spring, and built a sawmill a couple o' miles thataway. They were workin' here until last week. We've spent the summer building all this, and haying the land, and puttin' in several miles o' split-rail an' pole fencing around pastures and corrals. I'm heading for Mexico in two months, in early December, to buy horses. Most will go to the cavalry, but several hundred will come back here with me in the spring."

Jim's eyebrows shot up. "How did you fix up all that?"

"It's a long story." Walt opened a door. "This is your room. Make yourself comfortable. Outhouse is through that door," and he motioned to the end of the long corridor. "We run the bathhouse boiler every evening from about five until eight, to let everyone clean up – families first, then the hands. There'll be plenty of hot water."

"Never seen that on a ranch before."

"Neither had I, until we hit Parsons' place. He'd built a bathhouse for himself and his men, with a boiler to provide hot water. I decided to copy his, but I made it big enough for everybody to use, not just Nate an' I. We don't have piped water in each building yet – Nate'll fix that up this winter, while I'm away – but we bring it down an irrigation pipe from the hills above, and we bought a water tower an' windmill pump from the people who make them for the railways." He gestured at the huge wooden cistern, roofed with shingles, mounted atop a shallow slope on a framework of heavy beams, flanked by the windmill. "We got thirty thousand gallons anytime we need it, for drinkin', cookin' an' cleanin' up, and for firefighting if worse comes to worst. It's good water, too, clean an' tasty."

"I'll look forward to washing off the trail dust." Dunnett laid his saddlebags and holdall on the bed, opened a saddlebag, and handed Walt a familiar green-bound ledger. "There you are."

"Thanks. I'll put it in the office safe."

Dunnett followed him down the passage to a large, airy room containing two rolltop desks, several chairs, a bookcase, and four big cupboards. A couple of big glass-fronted display cases, on either side of a big stone fireplace, contained a large selection of firearms. The visitor crossed to look at them as Walt used a key to open a big, heavy safe, and slid the ledger onto a shelf.

"You sure got a lot o' guns in here. Why so many?"

"Not as many here as at Ames Transport in Pueblo. I keep the guns of anyone who tries to rob my wagon trains. Also, some of them came from Parsons' men, and from Bart Furlong's gang. If anyone I hire doesn't have a decent gun, I lend them a revolver an' rifle from my stock until they can afford to buy their own. Right now there's a lot of old cap-an'-ball revolvers, because a lot o' my men are buyin' the new cartridge guns. The stores don't give much as trades on cap-an'-ballers, so I give 'em a dollar or two and add their old guns to my stock."

"I get it. I traded in my old revolver a month back for this new Colt Single Action Army. I got Carlos Gove to sell me the third one to reach his shop. He refused to sell the first two, or he'd've had nothin' to show his customers." The two men chuckled as the lawman tapped the butt of the gun in his holster. "It ain't as fast to reload as your Smith and Wesson Russians, but it's real strong, and its .45 cartridge hits hard. Fits my hand well, too. What did Parsons carry?"

"He used a Thuer cartridge conversion of an Colt 1860 Army Model." Walt opened a glass-fronted door, took out the topmost revolver and handed it butt-first to the lawman. "When I set up a proper family funeral plot, I'll re-bury Rose there. I reckon I'll put Parsons' gun on her coffin, so she'll sleep easy, knowin' I killed the man who caused her death."

Dunnett couldn't help noticing the lingering pain in Walt's voice. He checked that the gun was unloaded, then cocked the hammer and held it back with his thumb as he tried the trigger. "Nice, smooth, light action on this piece. Reckon Parsons had it worked over."

"Yeah. He was real good with it, too, but that wasn't enough to save him in the end."

Jim handed back the revolver. "Tell me more about your trip to Mexico," he invited.

"Sure. Like a drink to get rid of the trail dust?" Walt waved a hand towards a tray on a sideboard, bearing a decanter and four glasses, as he replaced the gun. "It's good Tennessee sippin' whiskey. My sister and her husband sent me a barrel a couple of months ago."

"Can't say no to that."

Walt poured two generous helpings of the amber liquid. They toasted each other, and drank. Jim shivered as the liquor hit the back of his throat. *"Daaaang,* that's smooth! Better be careful. I might have to confiscate the rest of that barrel as evidence when I leave!"

Walt laughed as he motioned his guest to take a chair. "Nate'll give you an argument about that. I'm leaving it here, to see him through the winter. He's going to carry on with setup work while I go get our horse herd."

"What made you think o' lookin' for horses in Mexico?"

"Pablo Gomez gave me the idea. He's one of those I hired to help me find Parsons. He turned out to have a real smart head on his shoulders. When Isom decided to stay in New Mexico with his new wife, and Sam joined him there, I needed a sidekick to ride with me and watch my back. During the hunt for Parsons, Pablo proved he was the right man for the job. He saved me from a booby-trap Parsons set up to catch anyone prying into his papers."

"How did that work?"

Walt explained the dynamite-rigged cupboard Parsons had set up. "But for Pablo, I'd have opened the door without suspecting a thing, an' been blown to bits. Anyway, Pablo's from Mexico. We got to talking on the way back here. He reckons there's good horses to be had in Mexico, but most buyers are poorer there, so they sell for a lot less than you'd pay for the same animal up here. That started me thinking. I thought even harder when we stopped at Fort Union, before turning north. Y'see, the Army needs horses every year to resupply its cavalry regiments. They can't afford to pay high for them, but scrub cow ponies ain't good enough for them, and the mustangs ain't what they used to be."

"Those scrubs sure are cheap. Word is you can buy 'em in Texas for five to ten dollars a head. What's wrong with the mustangs?"

"There's not enough good ones left to meet the demand. Leaves the Army with a real problem. It wants the best cavalry mounts it can get, but can only afford to pay up to twenty-five dollars a head. That ain't enough for a good mustang nowadays, but if the Army pays more than twenty-five for better stock, then they can't afford to buy enough horses."

"Sounds like they can't win, with choices like that."

"Yeah. That's what I thought, too, after talkin' to the commanding officer at Fort Union. He reckons they'll need up to two thousand remounts to prepare for next year's campaign season, but they don't know where they'll find them. That gave me an idea. What about Mexican horses? If I can buy quality animals for eight to ten bucks a head south of the border, and deliver 'em to forts in southern Texas for twenty-five bucks a head, I can give the Army what it needs, make some money, and also buy good breeding stock for myself. That's why I took this summer to get this place up an' runnin'. It's coming along nicely. With Nate to supervise the finishing touches over the winter, it'll be ready to take in several hundred horses come spring.

"I set up the contract with the Army over the summer, then sent Pablo south two weeks ago, with good men to back him and enough money to start things moving. He's putting in two thousand dollars of his own money, too, hopin' to double it or better. He's scouting out the best places to buy horses, an' passing the word to towns and ranchers south of the border. We'll go to several towns through the late winter. Sellers will know when to meet us there. We'll buy as many horses as we can. I'll have my men drive them from each town to El Paso or an Army fort, hirin' Mexican hands to help if they need 'em. Army horse doctors and farriers will inspect them when they get there, and buy those that meet their needs. I hope to move up to a thousand every month, in three to four smaller herds. We'll vary our routes so as not to overgraze the trail."

"How many men in all?" Jim asked.

"I reckon I'll need up to fifty. I'm taking ten of my own. Pablo's lining up more to join us in El Paso, and in Mexico. We'll also have a dozen or so Navajos that Isom's sending from New Mexico. His father-in-law's coming along, to boss them. They'll be our scouts, one or two with each group. They're also bringing some youngsters, to help handle the horse herds. Those beeves you saw roasting outside are to welcome them. They're due here today."

The lawman frowned. "You're taking them off the reservation? Won't that cause trouble?"

"I got Isom to arrange it, all legal an' proper, with a letter from the Reservation Agent confirming they have permission to work for me. They all speak some Spanish, and some know a few words in English. Thing is, they don't want payment in money. They want some o' those good Mexican hosses to improve their herds."

Jim nodded. "I hear the Navajo breed real good horses."

"They sure do! Some are descended from the original stock the Spanish brought with them. Nastas' family – that's Isom's father-in-law – has bred that line as true as they can keep it. He's bringing a couple o' dozen head of prime breeding stock, including one of his best stallions, to inject new blood into my herd. I'll give him three of those we bring back, of his choice, for every one he brings me. His scouts will get four hosses apiece, and the herd boys two. Apart from that, they'll work for their keep, plus five dollars a month spending money."

"Sounds like a good deal for both sides."

"They seem to think so, and it saves me a few hundred a month in wages, so I ain't complainin'."

"How many horses d'you think you'll get?"

"I'm hoping for up to two thousand for the Army, plus three to five hundred for myself, if I can find that many good ones."

Jim whistled in astonishment. "So you'll pay up to twenty-five thousand for them, and make up to fifty thousand from the Army. After your expenses, that should clear you a decent profit, and you'll have your breeding stock to boot. Not bad at all!"

"That's what I hope. If we do well, the profit on the horses will pay for all I've spent this year on setting up this ranch. 'Course, there's bound to be problems."

"Given the way you dealt with Parsons and his men, I reckon you'll handle 'em."

"I'll drink to that!"

They drained their glasses, and Walt refilled them. "I reckon you didn't come to see me just to give me that ledger," he observed as he re-stopped the decanter.

"Yeah. I need your help over the next few years."

"How?" They sat down again.

"I'm going to be lookin' into labor troubles on the mines. Some o' the miners' unions are workin' across state lines, which makes it Federal business. I'm also goin' to be keepin' my eye on competition between rival railroad outfits. Looks like there might be trouble brewin'. To do that, I'm goin' to build up a network of contacts in the mining towns. I need a way for them to get messages to me. That's where your transport company comes in.

"I'm gonna set up an office in Pueblo. If I ain't there myself, someone else will be. I figure, if your wagonmasters will accept routine messages from my contacts, then bring them back to your depot in Pueblo, you can pass 'em on. I can send messages back the same way. That'll be real secure. No-one will know about it. If they've got something urgent to tell me, they can send a telegram to Ames Transport in Pueblo, usin' some sort of code. If they use a code word you recognize, you'll know to bring the telegram to me right away. Will you help me out?"

"Sure, I'll do it. You helped me get Parsons, so it's the least I can do in return."

Jim relaxed in his chair. "Thanks, buddy. I reckoned I could rely on you. I know you won't blab about it, like some would."

"We'll set it up so no-one knows you're involved, apart from Samson and myself. He's my depot manager in Pueblo, and he'll forward messages and telegrams to you when I'm not there."

"I remember him. I met him last year."

"That's right, you did. All right, let's figure out the details."

3

It was mid-afternoon before a loud call from a lookout in the hayloft of one of the barns announced the arrival of the Navajo party. Their dust cloud could be seen from a couple of miles out, about a dozen riders plus several times that many horses. Some of the ranch hands gathered in the space between the buildings to welcome them, while families congregated on the porches, buzzing with curiosity.

Two men led the Navajos, and Walt smiled and waved as he saw them. Nastas, a big, imposing man, was flanked by Sam Davis, a former buffalo soldier who'd joined Walt's transport company shortly before Rose had been killed. He'd been part of the group that hunted down those responsible, and ended their threat forever. Since then he'd remained in northern New Mexico with Isom Fisher, another former buffalo soldier, Walt's second-in-command during the search. Isom had married Nastas' daughter, whom they'd rescued while on their mission. Walt had made over to them another of Parsons' properties as a home for themselves and her extended family, and Sam had stayed on to help them run it. Nastas had brought his breeding herd over from the Navajo reservation. The horses he and his men were riding and driving were mute evidence that it was doing well in its new home.

The new arrivals cantered through the main entrance to the ranch compound amid cheers and cries of welcome from those awaiting them. They drove their horse herd into a big corral set aside for them, with heaps of hay and full water troughs standing ready. They swung down from their mounts and off-saddled them as Walt shook hands with Nastas.

"Greetings, my friend," he said in Spanish to the grinning Navajo. "Is all well with you?"

"All is very well," Nastas assured him. "I see Pablo has taught you a lot more Spanish since we last met."

"He sure has. I wouldn't be goin' to Mexico without that. You brought lots o' hosses."

"We have twenty-four fine horses for you, and your friend Isom and my daughter Doli send greetings. Their first child was born last month – a boy. Isom calls him David, after his father, but we Navajo call him Shiyé."

"I'll send a gift for him with you when you return," Walt promised, and turned to Sam, switching to English. "How are you, Sam? Enjoying life out there with Isom?"

"Sure am, boss. We're runnin' more'n eighty head of horses now, since Nastas brought his herd from the reservation. Isom's got a couple dozen steers an' cows. We had a real good harvest, so he's gonna trade hay an' corn for as many yearling calves as he can get over the winter, to build up a small herd. He's raisin' pigs, too. They're good eatin'. About half the Mexican workers that were on the place before have stayed. They're farmin' a couple o' hundred acres, along with the Navajo women. They did real well with vegetables this year. When we left, they was cannin' and preservin' the harvest fit to beat the band, so there'll be plenty o' good food over the winter. They said they was pleased to get rid of us, 'cause there'll be more food for them!" Both men chuckled.

"You haven't found yourself a Navajo wife yet?"

"No, boss, but that ain't because some of 'em ain't tryin'! I wouldn't mind, but I ain't found one yet that I like enough for that. Who knows? Mebbe I'll find me a nice gal down in Mexico, to take home with me."

"Might happen. Just remember, the men down there may have their own ideas about that – and they favor knives. Watch your back."

Walt turned back to Nastas, and switched to Spanish again. "Please introduce me to your men."

"Of course." Nastas barked an order, and his dozen followers closed up together. He led Walt down the line. "This is Ahiga, my first-born son. He leads in my place when I am absent. Then there are our scouts; Kai, Niyol, Gaagii, Sik'is, Bidzii, and Tsela. These four boys are too young to serve as scouts, but will help handle our horse herds, and learn from the rest of us. It will stand them in good stead for the future. They are Ashkii, Naal-nish, Gad and Notah."

Walt ran his eyes over the Navajos as they were introduced. All wore a blend of cowhand trousers and Navajo-patterned shirts. Their feet were shod in calf-length moccasins, rather than boots, and their long hair was held back by headbands. Most of the scouts wore belts bearing a revolver on one side, and a knife or tomahawk on the other. Their saddles bore rifles and carbines. A few were repeaters, but most were older breech-loading single-shot weapons.

"Nastas, I see that one scout doesn't have a revolver, and none of the boys have guns."

"That is so. The guns you gave us last year, when you rescued Doli, were not enough for everyone. We hope to buy more while working for you."

"I can fix that. Tomorrow morning we'll issue guns to those that need them, including your herd boys. They may not be scouts, but there'll surely be those who want to steal our horses, and I'd like them to be able to defend themselves. I mostly have cap-an'-ball handguns and single-shot Sharps carbines, but they're a lot better than nothing. If you wish, over the next two months before we leave, we'll teach those who don't know how to use a handgun."

"Thank you. I will join them. I need to learn more. We have had more practice with rifles than with the small guns."

Walt made a mental note to send for a lot more cartridges, lead, powder, and bullet molds. With so many people to train, he'd need thousands of rounds. From the look of them, he'd also need to provide warm coats, gloves, and thick blankets, to make the trip south in the middle of winter more bearable. Ames Transport could bring everything from Pueblo.

"All right," he said. "I'll have our leatherworker make up holsters and belts for those who need them. Meanwhile, we've set aside one section of the bunkhouse for you and your men. Nate – you remember him – will take you there. We have hot water for baths, and two oxen are almost ready to eat. Tonight is fiesta time for everyone, to celebrate your safe arrival."

That evening the oxen were carved into heaping plates of food, their carcasses shrinking like snow melting on a hot rock in high summer, accompanied by vegetables, seasonings, and heaps of tortillas and johnnycake baked by a relay of grinning wives and daughters of the ranch hands. Walt had discouraged alcohol, strongly supported by Nastas. They knew what it could do to stomachs and heads unaccustomed to it – and besides, it was against the law to serve alcohol to Indians. Instead, he'd arranged a supply of water, lemonade, sarsaparilla and small beer. No-one seemed to mind. The ranch workers used those among them who spoke Spanish as interpreters, and the two groups were soon mingling freely and animatedly swapping stories. An impromptu band struck up in one corner with guitars, castanets and a tambourine, and before long couples were dancing in the dusk.

Jim Dunnett grinned as he stood with Walt on the porch of the administration building, both holding plates as they watched the festivities. "Dang, there must be fifty or sixty people here, old an' young, men an' women, white, black, Mex an' Injun, all havin' a helluva good time. I reckon you've started somethin' real good here, Walt."

"I've surely tried. In my transport business and here on the ranch, work can get real dangerous sometimes. We depend on each other to stay alive and out o' trouble. The real question about a man, the only important one, is whether he'll be there for us when we need him. I pick my people real careful, for that reason, an' make sure they see it that way as well – their families, too, for the married folks. Other differences just ain't as important."

"You'll be takin' a mixed bunch south, then?"

"Sure will. Anyone who doesn't like the idea will be fired as soon as I find out. Saves trouble down the road for the rest of us."

THE NEXT MORNING was a bustle of activity.

Walt began the day by calling together all those he planned to take to Mexico with him, the Navajos and ten of his own hands. "We've got about two months before we leave," he told them. "During that time we'll break all the new stock to saddle an' harness, slowly and gently, and finish most of the work of settin' up this place for the winter. Also, the Navajo will take a couple of weeks to visit Blanca Peak, south of here. It's one of four mountains they reckon are sacred to their gods, so it'll be a sort of pilgrimage. Some of them may stay there for longer.

"We leave for El Paso on the first of December. We're goin' to be coverin' thousands o' miles over the next few months; six hundred or so from here to El Paso, then better than two hundred an' fifty more to Chihuahua in Mexico, or double that to Hermosillo for those who go there. Some will come with me from El Paso, through Fort Clark, then across the Rio Grande to

Mexico. That's the best part o' five hundred miles. From there it's better'n three hundred miles south to Monterrey an' Saltillo. Also, don't forget: once we get all the way down, we've got to ride all the way back again, herdin' hosses!"

A soft groan rose from his listeners, many of whom instinctively rubbed their rears in anticipation of the bruising miles ahead. Walt couldn't help grinning as he continued, "We'll change horses as often as we need to, but we're still gonna have to treat 'em carefully, and not push them too hard. We'll be travelin' for at least five months. By the time we get back here, you'll have covered five or six times the distance that a typical trail drive covers from Texas to Kansas. It'll be something to tell your grandchildren about."

"That's if we can still *have* children, after grindin' our butts down to a nub," one hand muttered, not very quietly. Laughter greeted his sally.

"That'll only be a problem if you don't fit your saddle," Walt retorted, to more amusement. "If that seems like too much ridin' for anyone, now's your chance to back out." He looked around, but no-one moved. "All right. First off today, we're gonna look at the breedin' stock the Navajos brought for the ranch. I've had a quick look already, and I'm real impressed. They've done us proud. After that, we'll look at the hosses Vicente an' his *mesteñeros* brought. I may buy some or all of them, if they're good enough.

"After that, I'm gonna issue guns to those Navajo who don't have them yet. Any of you who ain't satisfied with the guns you got now, this is your chance to get better ones without havin' to buy 'em yourself. Mine ain't the latest models, but they're all in good condition and dependable. Bring your old ones to the administration building, and swap them for my stock. Make sure your holsters an' rifle boots are in good condition, and get them repaired or replaced by our leatherworker if need be – also your belts, boots an' saddlebags. I want everyone to carry at least fifty rounds for his revolver, and double that for his rifle – more if you can. We'll be huntin' for fresh meat every day, an' there's bound to be those who'd like to steal our hosses. I don't aim to let them." There was a growl of agreement from the hands.

"Make sure your clothes for the trip are in good order. Pack tough, hard-wearin' duds, at least three full changes, includin' warm clothes, long underwear and two pair o' boots. Each o' my hands must choose a string of three mounts from our workin' horses. Check your string carefully. Make sure they're fit an' healthy, and have 'em re-shod. The blacksmith'll make up spare horseshoes, and a couple of you know how to cold-fit 'em if any hoss needs it on the journey south. Check your saddles an' bridles, and put right anything that's worn. Make sure your bedroll is warm enough to get through the winter, even if we have to sleep in snow. Send to Pueblo for anything you need to buy before we leave, and we'll ship it here. We won't be stoppin' on our way south, except to buy food now and again.

"We'll take twenty pack horses with us. They won't be heavy loaded, so they can keep up with us. Five will carry your bedrolls, so you don't load your own mounts too heavy. The rest will bear food an' gear, includin' oats an' nosebags to keep up the hosses' strength on the trail. I'll take two extra pack horses. Jimmy and Randy," and he indicated two gangling teenage boys, "are comin' with us to tend to my hosses an' gear and run errands for me, 'cause I'll mostly be too busy with other things." The boys flushed as all eyes turned to them for a moment.

"Nate and I will be workin' with the Navajo, teachin' them to use their handguns better. If any o' you want to join us, you'll be welcome. Otherwise, get ready for the hardest winter's work you've ever done, and are ever likely to do!"

∾

After agreeing to buy the dozen horses Vicente had brought to the ranch, Walt took him aside. "You know what I'm plannin' over the winter?"

"I heard you talk to the hands this morning, señor. I will tell you honestly, I am amazed. To plan so large... you must be talking about thousands of horses!"

"Two to three thousand, if all goes well. What I really need are men who are good judges of horseflesh. The Army's got strict standards of what it'll accept. If we bring back hosses that don't meet 'em, they won't buy 'em. I can't afford that. I need men who can look at a hoss an' make up their minds quickly whether he's what we want. They may have to look over several hundred horses in just a few days. Reckon your *mesteñeros* could handle that job?"

"Some of them have many years' experience in judging whether a mustang is worth keeping, or a cull to be released. They could do it. However, some will not want to work through the winter. They will want to spend that time with their families."

"How many d'you think might join us? I'll pay each man thirty a month and found – that's their food, ammo, an' lodgin' when we ain't sleepin' out under the stars – plus a bonus of two to three months' wages when the job's done. That'll depend on how well we do, of course."

"For that, señor, I think I can find you eight men, perhaps up to ten. Like me, they live in Las Cruces in New Mexico Territory, but that is not far from El Paso. I can bring them there when you are ready."

"Sounds good. What about you? Will you come? If you do, I'll make you one of my group bosses. They'll earn fifty dollars a month and found. At the end of the job, if it goes as well as I hope, each boss will get a bonus of up to five hundred dollars."

Vicente sucked in his breath audibly. "That is very good money, *señor*." Walt knew the bonus was probably as much as the profit he would make in six months' hard work, gathering mustangs. "I had planned to stay with my wife and children over the winter, but for so much, I think she will understand if I leave after *Navidad* instead. Ah... may I bring one thousand dollars to invest in this venture? If it goes as well as you hope, it will help make up for a poor year's mustanging."

"That's all right with me. Meet me in El Paso on the first of January. It's a small enough place that you should find us with no problem. We'll be somewhere outside town, near Fort Bliss. Pablo's gonna buy or rent a place for us to use as a base."

"I shall be there, *señor.*"

4

"I'll be damned if I've ever seen anything like it!" Sandy exclaimed as he reined in his horse at the lip of the Palo Duro Canyon. None of the ranch hands had seen the giant gash in the earth before. They sat in their saddles, the dust from their passage eddying around them in the breeze, staring in awe at the sight below them as the plains plummeted into the chasm.

"They reckon this is only a small part of it," Walt said slowly, as amazed as any of his men at the vista opening out before them. "They say it goes on for a hundred miles or more. I guess not many white men have been through here, 'cept maybe the cavalry. The Indians know it well, though. These are Comanche and Kiowa stomping-grounds. They ride down here from the Indian Nations every spring and summer to hunt buffalo, and raid for horses and other loot. They're gonna be our biggest headache goin' back. A big herd of horses is gonna draw them like flies to honey." There was a rumble of somber agreement from the hands.

Nastas had learned enough English to understand the gist of what Walt had said. In Spanish, he asked, "Then why come back this way, brother? Why not stay to the west, and come up through what you whites call the *Llano Estacado,* the Staked Plains, or even further into New Mexico?"

"I'm considering that," Walt admitted. "Problem is, there ain't a lot of water or grazin' in that part o' the world. We'll be drivin' several hundred head o' breeding stock. I want to keep them in good condition, but they wouldn't be after a few weeks of short rations an' that nasty brackish alkali water."

Nastas laughed. "You brought us along, remember? We can scout for good water and the best grazing. If you wait until spring – say, early April – the grass will already be growing. We can lead you over the safest route, and avoid Comanche or Kiowa hunting and raiding parties. They will be after the buffalo herds, but most will stay to the east of the *Llano Estacado,* where the grazing and water are better."

"You may be right." Walt looked around at the relatively flat plain surrounding them. "The reason I took this road south is to check the grazin' conditions. Also, at this time o' year, the buffalo herds ain't here, so the Comanche and Kiowa have little reason to hunt; and the poor grazing means they can't raid too far from their homes. During spring or summer, it'd be more'n our lives are worth to use the Comanche Trail like this, drivin' a hoss herd without an Army escort. That's how the Trail got its name, after all."

Sam added, "That's why all this land's still open and not settled. Clear out the Injuns, and cattlemen will be all over the Texas Panhandle. We've traveled for days to get here, and ain't seen a single cow or even one ranch. There must be millions of acres just waitin' to be used."

"You'd have to clear out the buffalo as well," Walt pointed out. "They eat all the grass. The skin-hunters have already shot a lot, but there must be hundreds of thousands still in the southern herd."

Sam spat in disgust. "Yeah, but if them damned skin-hunters carry on like this, there won't be. Remember all the buffler skeletons we saw further north? They musta killed thousands last year, and they woulda killed more if there hadn't been so many Injuns around. They don't even take the meat – just the hides. They leave everythin' else to rot. They'll be back come summer, with them long-range rifles o' theirs, to do it all over again. It's no wonder the Injuns hate 'em. Can't say I blame 'em for feelin' that way."

Walt nodded silently, reflectively. At Fort Union, he'd noted a general sentiment among the officers and men that the more buffalo killed, the better, so as to deprive the Indian tribes of their sustenance and force them onto reservations. They relied on the buffalo for food, and hides to make their tepees and other necessities. Without them, their present wild, free way of life could not continue... and that would also end their incessant raids and cruelties to others.

Another Navajo scout, Niyol, had been looking around the horizon. He said slowly, "I cannot see anyone, but I have a feeling we are being watched."

"Es posible," Nastas admitted. "There could be a small raiding party nearby. Some braves get bored sitting around the fire over winter, doing nothing. They prefer to raid while there are few others competing with them, so the pickings are better. Our horses would make them rich, if they could steal them."

"Es verdad, amigo," Walt agreed. "We'll have to keep our eyes peeled. Double guards tonight, do you think?"

"I think that would be wise. There is another thing. *Comancheros* come up from Mexico to trade with the Indians. There may be some of them around. We must watch carefully."

"Let's do that. Have your scouts form a screen a few miles ahead of us, two by two. If anyone sees anything, one scout must stay on it while the other comes back to warn us. Also, let's not fire any shots unless we have to, so as not to draw attention to ourselves. D'you reckon your scouts could hunt for meat with their bows an' arrows instead?"

Nastas snorted. "Can a bird fly? Can a fish swim? Of course we can!"

Walt had to laugh. "All right, *amigo*. We'll leave meat for supper, an' breakfast too, in your hands." He turned to the others. "We've seen the canyon, and we've still gotta get round this end of it and make another ten miles before we camp for the night. Let's ride!"

THE SCOUTS KILLED a deer for supper. They led the group into a hollow, where the flames of their fires would not be visible across the plains, and tethered the horses. Everyone carved pieces of meat from the deer and threaded them onto twigs and improvised skewers, roasting them over the coals. Johnnycake baked in cast-iron skillets helped make it a filling meal, rounded off with black coffee strong enough to stain their enamel mugs.

"Wish we'd brought a chuckwagon along," one of the ranch hands groused. "We coulda had stew, an' pie, an' -"

Walt cut him off short. "It couldn't keep up if we have to move fast. A chuckwagon's fine for a cattle drive, but not for a hoss herd. Better for us to ride greasy sack like this, with our food on pack horses or huntin' for it, and small groups cookin' their own."

"Iffen you say so, boss." The hand sounded unconvinced, but didn't raise the point again.

Walt watched with interest as the Navajo prepared three wild turkeys they had shot with arrows. They didn't bother to pluck them, but slit open the stomach cavities and removed the entrails. Next, some of the scouts slathered each bird with moist clay that they dug out of the bed of a small creek, working it deep into the feathers. Others built a long, narrow campfire on an open strip of earth. When each bird resembled a ball of clay, they swept the fire to one side, dug down into the earth and buried the birds.

They then swept the coals back on top of them, and added wood to build up the fire once more.

"What's the idea with that?" Walt asked Nastas.

The Navajo grinned. "That is our breakfast."

The fire was allowed to die down when the men went to sleep. The following morning, the scouts dug up the birds. The clay had been hardened overnight by the residual heat of the coals, and the turkeys had cooked inside their protective shell. When it was cracked and removed, the feathers came off with the clay, and a delicious smell of baked turkey wafted over the campsite. Three large turkeys, along with the last of the johnnycake from the night before and fresh-brewed coffee, provided breakfast for twenty-five hungry travelers. They praised the scouts to the skies.

Grinning with pleasure at the compliments coming their way, six scouts swung into the saddle. Two would ride ahead, two to the left and two to the right of the main body, all six remaining in distant sight of each other and scanning for any potentially hostile presence. When everyone had finished eating, they cleaned their utensils, packed up, and prepared to follow the scouts. They all took fresh horses from their strings, letting those they'd ridden yesterday run free with the remounts.

Walt held the pace down to an easy walk, interspersed with short periods at a trot or canter to stretch the horses' muscles. Given how much riding lay ahead, and how much distance they'd have to cover over the next few months, he reckoned twenty miles a day was a fair rate of progress. It was fast enough to reach El Paso by his self-imposed deadline, but slow enough not to over-stress the horses. They fell into their usual formation on the march, one group in front, the remounts and pack horses following, and another group of riders bringing up the rear.

The afternoon was drawing on, and the sun slowly descending towards the western horizon, when they noticed one of the scouts, to the right of the column, heading in their direction at a gallop. Walt halted the main body and waited for him to come up. He slid his horse to a halt in front of Nastas, and gabbled something in Navajo.

Nastas fired a couple of questions back at him, then turned to Walt. "Tsela says there are two wagons and a dozen men camped in a hollow about six miles ahead. There are barrels set on planks beside the wagons, and mugs too. The men are heavily armed, and watchful. They guard their wagons and horses carefully. He thinks they are *Comancheros.*"

Walt nodded thoughtfully. Pablo had told him of the activities of the traders from northern Mexico, who brought guns, ammunition, whiskey and other trade goods to exchange with the Comanche and Kiowa for goods they had looted, horses, hides, and anything else that might be worth money. They were generally regarded as renegades by Americans, who hated and despised them for arming the Indians who preyed on settlers and travelers. In particular, supplying alcohol in any form to Indians was strictly forbidden under United States law. Those found doing so were subject to heavy prison sentences – if they weren't simply shot out of hand when caught in the act.

Walt twisted around to look at his men, who'd closed up to hear the scout's report. "Looks like *Comancheros* ahead. I aim to make sure o' that first, but if they are, I reckon we'll be doin' a public service to deal with 'em. Besides, they've got barrels out next to their wagons. If they hold whiskey, we sure don't need a bunch of stunk-up drunk or hung-over Comanches on our trail. What d'you say, boys?" There was an immediate chorus of agreement.

Walt turned to Nastas. "Can your scouts get any closer, to check on what's in the wagons, and make sure they're *Comancheros?* I don't want to hit them if they're just passin' through."

"*Si,* we can do that when it grows dark."

"All right. Have a couple of other scouts find us a place to bed down, not too far from those wagons, but far enough away they won't hear or see us. We'll settle down for the night, keep watch over them, and plan to hit 'em at dawn."

They slowed the pace to a steady walk and spread out, so as not to raise a dust cloud that might betray their presence. They watered the horses and filled their waterskins at a convenient stream, then waited for the sun to set. As dusk descended, the scouts led them slowly and quietly to the side of a low hill, about a mile from the wagons. The horses were picketed out of sight from the hollow.

"No fires tonight," Walt ordered. "We don't want the light of flames or coals, or the smell of smoke or food cookin', to give us away. Picket the hosses, then make a meal of jerky, dried fruit and nuts, and other trail food you can eat without cookin' it. Double sentries again. We'll be up two hours before sunrise, so the scouts can lead us over there in the dark. We'll take 'em at dawn. Make sure your guns are clean, full loaded and ready to use before you sleep."

Walt cleaned his revolvers, then prepared his gunbelt. He'd worn only one gun on his strong side while traveling, keeping the second in a saddle holster; but now he slipped a second, cross-draw holster onto his belt, and put his second revolver into it after cleaning and reloading it with fresh ammunition. He did the same for his primary weapon, then went over to his two pack saddles.

The youngsters, Jimmy and Randy, watched with bright-eyed interest as he looked thoughtfully at the long guns carefully strapped to one of the saddles, then selected a Remington Rolling Block sporting rifle. It was chambered in .50-70 Government, a hard-hitting round that could reach out for hundreds of yards to bring down the biggest game. He hefted it in his hands, remembering the snap shot he'd made with it to bring down the horse and stop the escape of the man who'd killed his wife. He'd made sure Parsons would never again prey on innocent victims.

As he took out a box of ammunition for the rifle, Randy

asked, "Boss, why the Remington? It's just a single-shot. Why not your Winchester carbine? It holds a lot more rounds, an' if you're gonna get into a fight, you may need 'em."

"Sure, but what if one of them makes a run for it? That little carbine's accurate enough at a hundred yards or so, but not much further. With this, I can hit him at four or five times that range."

"What about us, boss?" Jimmy asked.

"You're both stayin' with the hosses." Walt held up a hand to stop their immediate, instinctive protest. *"Don't argue with me!"* He looked at them for a moment, then squatted on his heels to bring himself down to their level as they sat on the ground, faces outraged at the thought of being left out. "I know you want to be there, boys, but this ain't no game. Jimmy, you're thirteen. You ain't got no parents to take care of you, so I reckon that puts me in their place right now. Randy, you're fourteen. I promised your Ma I'd take care of you – and that sure don't mean I'm gonna put you in danger without good cause!

"Neither of you is good enough with a gun – at least, not yet – to put you in the firin' line. Given more practice, you will be; but you still got a lot to learn. Besides, a real fight ain't like shootin' at a tree stump, or something that can't shoot back. The first time, you're gonna be real scared and on edge. You'll prob'ly make mistakes. I know I did! I can still remember my first shootin' fight, back in the War. I was damned lucky to get out of it alive. I want to make sure you know enough, and can handle your guns well enough, to survive yours."

"But what about the Navajo boys?" Randy demanded.

"Nastas will do the same with them as I'm doin' with you."

"You just don't trust us!" Jimmy fumed.

"That's crap, an' you know it!" Walt snapped; then, remembering his own younger days and how he'd felt about adults back then, his voice grew softer, gentler. "I *need* you here, boys. I'm gonna leave a couple o' men behind, too, even though I'll need 'em if this comes to a fight. We're relyin' on you all to bring up our mounts when the shootin' stops. If any Injuns are close enough to hear the fight, they're gonna come lookin' for trouble, and we'll need our hosses to get out of it. That's a real important job. If I didn't trust you, I wouldn't let you do it."

Slowly, reluctantly, the boys conceded his point. Walt offered a carrot to go with the stick of his refusal. "If you boys do a good job in the mornin', we'll make time on the ride south for some more practice, and do the same in El Paso. Just remember – don't go tryin' to take a fight to anyone who doesn't really need it. He gets a vote, too, an' he may be better with a gun than you are. You don't want to find that out the hard way unless you got no other choice."

Walt took Nastas aside, and they planned the morning's activities carefully before going to sleep. When the scouts woke the camp at three-thirty the following morning, they called everyone together, and briefed them.

"The scouts will lead us across the mile or so of ground between us and them," Walt began. "We'll be on foot." A low moan came from his ranch hands, many of whom had brought only high-heeled riding boots, which were not comfortable for extended walking. "Yeah, I know you'd rather ride, but they're more likely to hear horse hoofs, and our mounts might neigh when they get scent o' their hosses. Better to walk quietly.

"The scouts will ease you all into position around the rim of the hollow, a bit back from the edge so you won't be skylined against the light of dawn. Stay as quiet as you can. Pick a bush in front of you along the rim. Soon as there's light in the sky, move forward so the bush breaks up the outline of your head and shoulders as you look down. No sense in giving them an easy target. Four scouts will be mounted, and wait on the far side of the hollow. They'll go after any *Comancheros* who try to run for it.

"I'll start the ball rollin' by callin' on them to surrender. If they do, we let them, you hear me? Keep 'em covered, and don't trust 'em. Wait until they've been disarmed and secured, then you can come down; but don't rely on that happenin'. We know they're *Comancheros,* because the scouts sneaked right up to their camp last night. Those barrels hold rotgut whisky, an' the wagons are full o' guns, ammunition and trade goods. That bein' so, they'll probably fight; or, if they run, they'll meet up with their Injun friends and bring 'em after us. We can't risk either. If they don't surrender right off, put 'em down fast and hard.

"Don't none of you sample that snakehead whiskey, either! First thing we'll do after we take their camp is tip those barrels over an' empty them into the dirt." Another anguished moan arose from some of his men. "I know you'd like a drink, but that stuff'll poison you or send you clean off your head, so we ain't gonna use it. That's final. Anyone who does, I'll fire him right here, right now, an' he can make his own way back, alone, through Injun territory – if he survives." The determination in Walt's voice made it clear he wasn't joking.

"What about what's in the wagons?" a hand asked.

"We'll worry about that when we've taken 'em. I reckon every man deserves a share. You know I'm a fair man. I'll see everyone gets theirs." A rumble of agreement and assent.

"Any more questions?" Silence. "All right. The boys stay here with the herd, and the Navajo boys as well. Smiler, Dave, I want you to stay with them, too. We'll saddle up the pack hosses an' mounts before we leave. When you hear the shootin' stop, bring all the hosses over there, quick as you can. If there are any Comanche or Kiowa close enough to hear the shots, they may come hornin' in, and I want us mounted and ready to meet them if they do. Now, make fast your saddlebags an' bedrolls, saddle your broncs, then let's get moving – *quietly!*"

WALT SLID SLOWLY, carefully, noiselessly up to the rim of the hollow, masking his movements behind a low bush as he stared downwards into the gloom. The first light in the sky had not yet penetrated the darkness below. There was only the glow of a small fire in front of the two wagons, the indistinct silhouette of one man on watch near it, and the slow, shadowy movements of large dark shapes where the *Comancheros'* horses were picketed. He forced himself to be patient as he wriggled into a better shooting position, brought his rifle up to his shoulder, and settled down to wait.

As the light slowly grew, he could make out more of the camp below. Four of the men slept on the ground beneath each wagon, with the remaining four between them. One of the bedrolls in the center was empty, presumably that of the sentry sitting sleepily next to the fire. He was staring into the coals, which made Walt shake his head. The man was destroying his night vision by doing that; a betrayal of his comrades, but a welcome improvement to the attackers' chances of bringing this off.

At last Walt judged there was light enough to see their rifle sights and hit their targets. He took a deep breath, then shouted aloud in a commanding voice, *"Muévete y mueres!* If you move, you die!"

There was an instant flurry of activity as the men kicked their bedrolls away and grabbed for the guns lying beside them. Clearly, they were in no mood to obey – and that suited Walt fine. He had already aimed at the sentry, who was the only man already armed and capable of immediate resistance. As the man sprang to his feet, looking around wildly, he squeezed the trigger of his rifle. The big, heavy slug punched into his target, slamming the *Comanchero* down flat across the embers of the camp fire. He was dead before he knew what hit him.

On either side of Walt, firing erupted as his men opened up on the *Comanchero* band. Within seconds, more than half of the group had fallen. However, the rest didn't try to surrender. Instead, they made a run for the horses, picketed on the far side of the fire.

"*Páralos!* Stop them! Don't let them get away!" Walt bellowed as he fed another fat .50-70 cartridge into the chamber of his rifle. He closed the breech and squinted through the sights, aiming at the figure closest to the horses. His rifle boomed. The *Comanchero* arched his back and screamed as he fell forward. The two men behind him fared no better, attracting slugs from several of the rifles on the rim above. They joined their comrade in sprawled-out death.

Just one *Comanchero* made it to the horses. He slashed at a picket rope with his knife, swung astride bareback, and kicked his heels into the horse's ribs. Already startled by the gunfire, it sprang forward. Showing great skill, the rider stayed astride despite the lack of reins or stirrups, steering the horse by leaning to one side or the other as it raced up the far slope towards safety. Several of the men fired at him, but could not hit the fast-moving target in the gloom.

He'd almost made it when Nastas appeared on the rim, not fifty feet ahead of him. The big Navajo reined in his horse, aimed the Winchester 1866 rifle that Walt had given him after rescuing his daughter, and fired a single shot that struck the oncoming rider full in the chest. He clutched at the wound, screaming, and tried desperately to turn the horse; but by then Walt had reloaded and drawn a bead on him. The big four-hundred-and-fifty-grain soft lead bullet swatted the *Comanchero* from the horse's back as if he were no more than a fly. His body bounced and rolled back down the slope as Nastas caught his horse by the rope trailing from around its neck.

"Hold your fire! *Hold your fire!*" Walt yelled. Other voices took up the cry, and the guns along the rim fell silent as they stared down at the bodies below. "Reload your guns, then let's walk down there and make sure they're dead. Be real careful, in case one of 'em's playing possum. If he is, shoot him again – but don't hit each other!"

He tucked the big rifle into the crook of his left arm, with his hook through the trigger guard to hold it in place; then he drew a revolver with his right hand, and started down the slope. On either side, his men followed his lead. As they drew nearer, some of the Navajo scouts hurried to calm the whinnying, plunging horses at their picket line. They'd first been shocked out of sleep by the gunfire, then disturbed by the approach of strangers. Clearly, they were anything but pleased with their rude awakening.

While the others checked the bodies, Walt picked up an axe lying next to a small pile of firewood. He walked over to the first barrel, resting on a plank lying across two stones, and smashed open the head of the cask; then he kicked it off the plank to lie on its side, its contents gurgling away into the sandy soil. He wrinkled his nostrils at the sudden stench of cheap snakehead alcohol as he did the same to the remaining two barrels. It mingled with the smell of burning flesh and clothing from the sentry, who was still lying across the coals of the fire. Walt gestured in sudden irritation. "Drag that body off o' there!"

Two of the men obeyed, while the rest watched in silence as the liquid spread across the soil, sinking in. Within a minute, it had all been absorbed. Walt sighed with relief. He knew how great the temptation would have been for some of his men – but that was no longer a factor.

"All right, let's see what's in the wagons," he ordered. "Sam, Ahiga, check that one. Nastas, let's you and I look over this one."

The wagon proved to contain many trade items such as axe heads, knives, cloth and cookware. The most useful, to Walt's mind, were three dozen brand-new wool blankets, red in color, soft, thick and warm.

Sam straightened up in the other wagon, and yelled, "Boss, you gotta see this!"

"Coming!" he called, and jumped down from the wagon. As he approached, he asked, "What is it?"

"These carrion had two dozen Winchester 1866's, and half a

dozen of the new iron-framed Model 1873's. I heard o' them, but never seen one afore – they ain't made it to our part of New Mexico yet. There's lots of ammunition for them, too."

"Waal, I'll be damned! I've got an 1873 carbine on order back in Colorado, but it hadn't reached me before we left. They've only just started hittin' the stores. Where the hell did *Comancheros* lay their hands on them?"

"Dunno, but there's two carbines here, boss, and four rifles. Looks like a couple thousand rounds of .44-40 centerfire shells for them, too. The '66's are all rifles, an' there's prob'ly four, five thousand .44-28 rimfire rounds for them."

"Looks like we hit the jackpot," Walt said with a grin. "All right, soon as the hosses get here, we'll see who needs what."

When everyone had arrived, and the horses had been brought down into the hollow, Walt called everyone together to tell them what they'd found in the wagons. "All o' you should take one o' the new blankets in that wagon," he said, pointing. "Just one, mind! I'll have the extras put on pack horses to take with us. Some of those joining us at El Paso may need one. Also, if your belt knives ain't good ones, there's a couple dozen Green River knives in that wagon, with sheaths. If you need one, take one. I'm gonna add the rest of 'em and the cookin' pots to our load. After all that, take anything else you want, but don't weigh your hosses down with things you don't need.

"That wagon," and he pointed to the other one, "holds Winchester rifles; six of the brand-new Model 1873's, and twenty-four Model 1866's, the old brass-framed 'Yellow Boy'. I'm claimin' the two 1873 carbines, one for me, the other for Isom Fisher. Remember, he also lost a hand, and like me, he's fixed a ring under the fore-end of his carbine to let him manage it with his hook. The shorter carbines are easier for us to handle in rapid fire than the longer, heavier rifles. As for the four 1873 rifles, I'm allocatin' two to the Navajo, and two to my ranch hands. I'll leave it up to Nastas to figure out who gets them among his scouts. The rest of you can draw lots. The two winners get the rifles.

"Now, about those Yellow Boys. How many of you don't already own a Winchester?" Four hands went up from his ranch employees, and seven of the Indians. "Each of you gets one of the 1866 rifles, and plenty of ammo. Same goes for the herd boys." There were sudden whoops of excitement from the Navajo youths and his two young assistants, drawing laughter from the men. "Those who don't need a rifle, don't worry. I'll pay you the value of one of them when we get to El Paso, so you won't lose out."

"What about our old rifles?" one of his ranch hands asked.

"We're gonna take the *Comanchero* hosses with us. We'll use the wagon covers to make rough-an'-ready panniers and bundles that we can tie on to their riding saddles. They won't work as well as proper pack saddles, but we should be able to load bedrolls, sacks o' grain and other soft stuff on those hosses. You can use the space that frees up to load your old rifles on our pack saddles. You can sell 'em at El Paso."

"Great! Thanks, boss."

"All right. Sam, draw straws among our ranch hands for their two 1873 rifles; and Nastas, you figure out how to divide 'em among your scouts. We'll split the .44-40 ammo six ways. The rest, take a Yellow Boy if you need one, plus three hundred rounds of ammunition. That'll be enough for you to get to know the rifle, and leave some over to take to Mexico. The rest of the rifles and ammo, plus the *Comancheros'* weapons, will be loaded on our pack hosses once we've sorted out their saddles. Take all the food that's worth takin'. I'll get their money – I doubt they'll have much – and use it to buy more food an' such. Get your new blanket, plus a knife if you want one. Work fast! I want to move out in half an hour."

The group erupted into activity. The men who won the Model 1873 rifles were jubilant, whilst the losers groaned; but they were more than happy to accept older-model Winchesters instead. Walt noticed the Navajo scouts pressing one of the 1873's on Nastas, who didn't look as if he was resisting too hard. They drew lots for the remaining rifle, and then made a beeline for the wagon to get Yellow Boys for the other scouts and herd boys.

"What're you gonna do with the rest o' their stuff, boss?" Sam asked as they watched the men add the new blankets to their bedrolls.

"I thought o' burnin' it, but that'd make smoke. It'd be seen from miles off. I'd rather not attract more attention than we have to, so I'll leave it all here. Any Injuns finding it will loot the wagons an' count themselves lucky. I doubt they'll try to follow us."

"That oughta work, boss – and you've taken all the guns and ammo, so they won't end up better armed than they were before."

"That's the idea."

When all was ready, Walt swung into his saddle. "The shooting will have alerted any Indians within earshot. Let's get the hell out of here before they try to argue with us!"

With a rumble of hooves from the horse herd, now augmented by a score of captured animals, the group rode up the slope and disappeared over the rim, heading south towards Mexico. Behind them, the pillaged wagons, the empty barrels, and the still, silent corpses of the *Comancheros* were the only signs they had ever been there.

5

They arrived at El Paso shortly after Christmas. It was a cold, windy day. Everyone was huddled into their heavy jackets, some with blankets wrapped around themselves as well.

Walt halted his men just outside town, in the shelter of a small hill. "Wait here. Pablo was to leave word with the Wells Fargo agent about what he'd fixed up for us. I'll be back soon."

Sure enough, Pablo's initial message was waiting, as were six letters from him sent from various towns in Mexico, and a very eager agent whom he'd clearly paid well to be helpful. "That's right, Mr. Ames. Mr. Gomez bought the old Baker farm, just outside town. He got it for a real good price, 'cause old man Baker had just died an' his son didn't want to stay in El Paso. Here are the keys." He handed them over. "It's got a big barn and corral, with a full hay barn next to it, an' he bought a lot more hay and stacked it under tarpaulins. The house was run-down, but he paid a couple o' folks to clean it out and fix the roof, an' lay in plenty of firewood. Wexler's general store has ordered supplies for you, an' the feed barn has sacks of oats an' bran set aside for you. Mr. Gomez part-paid for them in advance – here's the bills and receipts. They'll deliver them by wagon, soon as you pay the balance."

"That's all very good. You've arranged the account facilities I need?"

"Uh... that's a problem, Mr. Ames. This is a small office. We don't have the same facilities as a big branch. I can take your gold on deposit, but I can't convert gold to greenbacks in the amounts Mr. Gomez mentioned, and I can't get San Antonio to send me that many banknotes."

"Then I guess I'll have to talk to the Army, an' see what I can fix up with them."

"Yes, sir. Ah... may I make a suggestion?"

"Sure."

"Mr. Gomez said you'd be buying horses in Mexico. Gold coin is at a premium in Mexico right now. Here in the U.S.A., a greenback dollar is valued at eighty-five cents, compared to a gold dollar; but deeper into Mexico, further from the border, it's more like sixty cents. If you offer gold, you can pay lower prices, and they'll likely jump at the chance to get hard money."

As a former Confederate soldier, Walt couldn't help smiling inwardly. The Union had printed greenback paper dollars, unsupported by gold reserves, as a way to expand the North's money supply during the war, and help defeat the South. The move had served its purpose at the time, but its consequences were still reverberating through the nation's financial system. Greenbacks were still trading at a discount to gold dollars, almost nine years after the war ended, and that looked set fair to continue for the foreseeable future. He contented himself with saying, "That's a good idea. Thanks. I'll consider it."

He tucked Pablo's letters into his pocket for later attention, and headed for the general store. The proprietor eagerly accepted the balance of the payment for the big order Pablo had placed, and promised to deliver it later that afternoon.

"Will you be needing to order more, Mr. Ames?"

"I sure will. I reckon I'll have fifty to sixty men here by soon after New Year's Day, an' we've got to stock up to head into Mexico." Walt passed a list across the counter. "How much o' that can you fill? If you can't, t'aint a big problem – I'll get it from Las Cruces."

"I deal with suppliers there, Mr. Ames. I can get you all of this, and have it here within four or five days."

Walt could almost hear the mental *ka-ching* of a cash register in Mr. Wexler's head. He couldn't help smiling. "Thanks. Order all that, then. There may be a follow-up order once all my men are here."

The feed barn was a different matter. The proprietor smiled unpleasantly as he said, "Prices have gone up. You owe me a lot more than that now."

Walt stiffened. "A deal is a deal, Mr. Eslin. You entered into a contract, and took money for it. I'm holdin' you to it."

"Too bad! Iffen you want your oats an' grain, you'll pay double what's outstandin' on that invoice, or I'm keepin' it all."

Walt shot out his hand, grabbed the front of Eslin's shirt and hauled him bodily over his own shop counter. Yelling in protest, the feed barn owner swung a wild haymaker. Walt avoided it, then landed a hard kick in the man's groin, doubling him over and sending him gasping and wheezing to the floor. He laid hold of his collar with the hook on his left wrist and dragged him out of the feed barn, then kicked him stumbling towards where he'd seen the mayor's office.

As they made their way down the street, people burst out of their shops and houses to goggle at what was going on. The town marshal yelled, "Hey! You! What the hell are you doin'?"

"I'm taking Mr. Eslin here to talk to the mayor."

"But you can't treat him like that!" The marshal's hand sank towards his holster.

Walt stopped dead in his tracks, turning to face the lawman, his own hand ready over his gun. "If you pull that, marshal, it'll

be the last thing you ever do. Instead o' fussin', why not come
down to the mayor's office with me, an' find out what's goin' on?"

"I... ah... Hey! Wait for me!"

Waving his hands helplessly in the air, the marshal followed
as Walt kicked and shoved Eslin onto the porch of the mayor's
office and through the front door. A big, burly man sprang to his
feet behind a desk.

"What the hell is this?"

Walt waited for the marshal to enter, then closed the door as
Eslin collapsed into a chair, half-sobbing, panting for breath. He
glanced at the nameplate on the desk. "Mayor Dowell, I'm Walt
Ames. Happen you've heard of me."

"Ah... yes, Mr. Ames. We heard you were coming to El Paso to
buy horses." The mayor was staring in undisguised fascination at
the steel hook on Walt's left wrist.

"Lots o' horses." Walt gestured towards the street outside
through the office windows, the view now almost blocked by
pointing, staring spectators. "Small town, this, Mr. Mayor. I'd
guess you've got less than a hundred fifty people, right? Maybe as
many again, or a few more, in the Mexican town across the Rio
Grande?"

"That's Paso del Norte. It used to be one town with this, until
we beat Mexico in the 1846 War an' the river became the
boundary 'tween it an' Texas. El Paso became a city just this year.
I'm its first city mayor."

"Uh-huh. A place this small needs business to grow. I've
brought twenty-five men with me, and there's a lot more comin'. I
was plannin' to spend thousands of dollars on Mexican hosses
over the next three, four months, based outta the old Baker place,
plus a lot more on supplies – but now this sonofabitch is trying to
cheat me." He tossed the invoice and receipt onto the desk. "My
advance party paid half up front. Now Eslin's tellin' me I have to
pay double the balance to get my goods. If that's the way your
shopkeepers are gonna treat us, I'll take all my money, an' all my

men an' their wages, an' all my business, and head for Las Cruces in New Mexico. It's a much bigger town, an' it's only two day's ride from here. I reckon they'll appreciate havin' a few thousand dollars in their pockets, rather than yours; an' I can arrange with the Army to do business through Fort Selden there, 'stead o' Fort Bliss here. What d'you say, Mr. Mayor?"

"Er... ah... I'm sure this is all a simple misunderstanding, Mr. Ames."

"Uh-huh. *Suuuure* it is. Tell you what. Explain to Mr. Eslin, and every other business in town, that happen there's another 'misunderstanding' like this, we'll be gone. Eslin, get my order out to the Baker place before sunset, at the original price, as agreed. Two wagonloads of oats an' grain, best quality, in sacks – and you make *damned* sure there's nothin' been taken out o' those sacks, an' dirt or gravel put in its place, you hear me? If I find anything like that, I've got a dozen Navajo scouts. I'll tell them you're the reason their hosses are gonna be short of grain, then I'll let 'em come lookin' for you. Believe me, you won't enjoy it when they find you."

The town marshal stiffened, clearly alarmed. "Injuns? You'd better keep them out o' town, mister. Folks round here had too much trouble with Comanches and Apaches, an' they won't stop to ask what tribe your scouts are."

"Sorry, marshal. They're here legally, with permission from the U.S. Government. That being the case, they'll come into town in small groups to shop. I'll send a couple o' my other men with them when they do, to sort out any problems. My scouts know it's illegal to sell whiskey to Injuns, so they won't try to go into the saloons. You just make sure they're treated fair, you hear me? I don't want to hear of anyone tryin' to make trouble for them, or my other men. You treat us right, and I'll do the same for you, and pay the fines for any of my men who get into trouble. On t'other hand, if you give them trouble for no good reason, I'll hear about it sooner or later, even if I'm outta town at the time. When I get

back, I'll be along to talk to you about it. You don't want to make
me do that."

"You can't threaten me!"

"Ain't threatening you, marshal. I never threaten. I make
promises – and I keep 'em." Walt's voice was cold, flat and hard.

"I'll pass the word to everyone, Mr. Ames," Mayor Dowell
promised. "With all the business you're bringing to town, they'll
understand."

Walt took his wallet from his pocket, extracted a dollar bill,
and tossed it on the mayor's desk. "While you're at it, buy a drink
for the marshal and yourself, and one for Mr. Eslin too. He looks
like he needs a pick-me-up. It'll help him remember not to try to
cheat me next time."

He turned on his heel and walked out. The three men stared
after him in stunned silence.

Walt's men were grinning as he rejoined them. From a
distance, they'd witnessed his handling of the feed barn owner.
He couldn't help smiling as he told them why he'd treated him so
roughly. His tale was received with loud laughter.

The Baker farm was only a mile or so out of town. They
turned their horses into the corral and barn while Walt walked
through the farmhouse, looking around, then issued orders.

"There's just barely enough room for all of us to sleep in the
house and the barn's hayloft. I get the bedroom in the house,
along with Jimmy and Randy. Four of you can sleep on the floor
in the main room. The rest of you, pick a spot in the hayloft, and
don't fight over it. The barn won't hold more than a dozen horses,
though, so put all ours in the corral. Carry all the saddles an' pack
saddles into the barn, to keep them out o' the weather."

He beckoned two of his ranch hands. "Shep, Miguel, you
helped build our hay barns and corrals this summer. I want more
corrals, to hold up to five or six hundred horses. Go into town, see
what poles an' timber are to be had, and come tell me the prices.
Ask at Wexler's store about tools and anything else you'll need.

Also, plan on roofed barns, open at the sides, to shelter all this hay. If we get a spell of real bad weather, tarpaulins won't be enough. We'll all turn to building them as soon as you get what we need."

By the time the two men returned, wagons from the general store and the feed barn had delivered all the supplies Pablo had ordered. Walt double-checked the feed store order, to make sure it hadn't been shorted or adulterated, and pronounced himself satisfied. He paid the balance due, then turned to Miguel while the others moved the supplies into the house and barn.

"We can get poles and tools in town, *señor,*" the ranch hand told him. "There are only enough planks and boards for one hay barn, but on the other side of town there are several old, half-collapsed buildings, long abandoned. I talked to the town marshal. He says the owners all left town years ago, so we should buy their wood from the town, tear them down, and bring it out here. That will give us the rest of what we need."

"All right. We'll go talk to the Mayor tomorrow morning, just to make sure he's all right with that, and that the price is right. Find me a good woodworker, too. I want him to carve a thicker fore-end for my new carbine, same as I did for my old one. It'll have to be of good hardwood, to take a ring that'll fit the end of my hook, so I can hold it tight into my shoulder.

"I'll borrow some tents from Fort Bliss tomorrow, for the rest of our people when they get here. Tonight, both of you figure out where you'll put the corrals, and divide the men into work parties. You're in charge of buildin' them, and puttin' roofs over the haystacks. Oh – build another four or five outhouses, too, well clear of the house and barn, and have the men dig holes under them. One just won't do for this many people, plus those we got comin'."

That evening, washing in ice-cold water from the well, Walt shivered, and made a mental note to unpack the *Comancheros'* iron pots and cauldrons. He'd have his men build a framework to suspend them over fires outside. Hot water for washing would be a very welcome thing in mid-winter temperatures. He also reminded himself to buy proper pack saddles and thick cushioning pads for the *Comanchero* horses. The ride down had proved that twenty pack horses were only just enough for long distances without resupply. The captured animals would double the size of his pack train, making the long ride through Mexico much easier.

Over supper, he resolved to hire a cook in town, or across the river in Paso del Norte, and have the hands expand the house's kitchen with a lean-to addition, big enough to cook for everybody. They'd all shared cooking duties on the ride down here, but no-one had been very good at it. Good food did more than almost anything else to boost morale and make everyone work harder. It would be well worth the expense.

VICENTE ROMERO BROUGHT eight men from Las Cruces on the first of January, 1874. Walt and those with him welcomed them warmly, both figuratively and literally, lighting a big bonfire that night and celebrating with a huge meal. The newly-hired cook dragooned some of the Mexicans into helping her, and served up a gigantic pot of chili with side dishes of beans and tortillas. It kept everyone's insides as warm as, if not warmer than, their outsides. She had already won their devotion by proving she could cook bacon and eggs, Anglo style, for breakfast, along with fried potatoes and other favorites. Relays of the hands washed the dishes and cookware after every meal.

The following day a dozen cowhands arrived, each leading extra horses. They'd been sent from the Gainesville area of northern Texas by Tyler Reese. Walt had met him while traveling westward through Kansas, back in 1866. Their paths had crossed as the rancher drove a herd north, from Texas to the railhead.

They'd kept in touch by mail ever since, even though separated by hundreds of miles.

"I'm Jess Manning," the leader of the group introduced himself. He was a tall, spare man, his face brown even in midwinter after many summers working cattle under the Texas sun. "I'm one of the trail bosses who take herds north for Tyler every year. He keeps us on over the winter, to plan for next trail drive season. I was gettin' bored, so when you arranged this with him, I jumped at the chance for a change of scenery."

"Glad to have you along." Walt couldn't help adding, with a grin, "You'll be workin' your butts off in the saddle for the next three months, so I ain't sure you'll want to ride north to Kansas again anytime soon."

Jess laughed. "If it pays well enough, we'll be there."

"This'll pay well enough, if we get it right. Did you have any trouble gettin' enough hands?"

"Not at the wages you're offerin', an' bonuses to boot if it all works out. In winter lots o' cowhands are laid off until the spring roundups, so we could take our pick o' the best around Gainesville. Tyler'll bring another ten with him when he meets you at Fort Clark in a few weeks."

Walt rubbed his hands – or rather, his hand and his claw – briskly together. "That's great! I'll need every one o' them. I'll call everyone together as soon as Pablo gets here, which should be any time now, and he'll tell us what's gonna happen next."

That very evening, as they were filling their plates with roast goat meat, beans and cornbread, Pablo and a dozen Mexican *vaqueros* rode wearily up to the farmhouse. As he climbed down from the saddle, Walt hurried to meet him.

"Pablo! Good to see you, *amigo*. There's lots o' food. Come eat, all of you, and we'll talk once you've got that inside you."

"Thank you, *señor*. My stomach was just asking me whether my throat had been cut!"

After the meal, while the new arrivals introduced themselves to the others and everyone relaxed over steaming enamel mugs of coffee, Pablo followed Walt into the farmhouse to report back. "It is done, señor," he began. "Everything is as you wished. I have made the grand circle from El Paso down to Chihuahua. From there I sent riders further south to Torreón, then across to Saltillo and Monterey. They will meet you at Fort Clark at the end of this month, to guide you. From Chihuahua I turned west to Hermosillo, then north to Nogales in Arizona, then east to come back here. Along the way, I sent riders to every town on either side of the trail, to pass the word of your interest in horses, and set up these horse fairs where they must bring them." He handed over a list.

"You've been workin' real hard," Walt observed, impressed, as he glanced over the list. "From the ranch, all that way, then back to El Paso... that's gotta be near on two thousand miles if it's an inch! You've been in the saddle more'n three months."

"*Si, señor*. I bought new horses in Hermosillo, because those we started with were too worn out to continue, even though we took good care of them. My *nalgas* are asking sorrowfully what they have done to offend me, to make me treat them so badly." Both men laughed.

"You tell your backside it can rest for a few months now. You'll be in charge here, receivin' the hoss herds, letting the Army inspect them, and handing them over in exchange for Government payment drafts. After that, they're the cavalry's problem."

"I cannot tell you how much I look forward to staying in one place for a while, *señor!* However, you will be covering almost as much distance yourself during that time."

"And I ain't lookin' forward to it, believe me! Still, if we make as much money as I hope we will, it'll be worth it."

"And get your breeding stock for your ranch as well, *señor.*"

"Yeah. That, too. All right, bed your men down in the tents outside. Tomorrow, you'll tell everyone what's gonna happen, and we'll split them up into teams."

THE FOLLOWING MORNING, Pablo used whitewash to paint a large square on the outer wall of the barn. The thin liquid dried quickly in the cold breeze, and he spent an hour drawing on it with burned sticks, making a map of northern, central and western Mexico. At last, satisfied, he called everyone together. Walt came to the front, and stood with him as he laid out the schedule for the next few months.

"We have arranged horse fairs in these towns," and he rattled off their names and the dates as he pointed to them on the map. "One of our teams will be in each town on that date, and for up to a week afterwards. Those who wish to sell horses know to meet them there. They or their riders may help you drive the horse herd to El Paso. The team leaders will hire more *vaqueros* at each place if they need them.

"Our Navajo scouts will be divided, one to each team. They will scout for grazing and water on the way down, and guide the herds to them on the way back. Each herd will follow a different route, so that they do not eat the grass those coming behind them will need. Being winter, there will not be good grazing, so we must be very careful about that.

"Each team will make two trips south and back again. The first will be deep into Mexico, to Hermosillo, Chihuahua and towns around them. I expect you will return from there with your horse herds by the end of February. At that time, you will go out again to towns nearer the border, to buy from farmers and ranchers there. You should be back from those trips by the end of March or early April. I think each team should be able to buy at least a hundred good horses at each stop, and perhaps more if all goes well.

"While we are doing that based out of El Paso, *señor* Ames will take his teams to Fort Clark, where more cowhands will join him. He will take them south to Monterrey and Saltillo, on the eastern side of Mexico. They will do there what we will be doing here. Because of the much greater distance, his teams will make only one trip down and back, but there are many horses in that part of the country, so they may be able to buy more there than we can here. They will deliver them to Fort Clark, then *señor* Ames will return here by the end of April."

Pablo fielded questions and comments for a few minutes, then handed over to Walt. He stepped forward, looking around the group of almost sixty men. "I told those of you who rode with me that this was gonna be the hardest-workin' winter you'd ever known. Now you know what I mean!" Laughter, mingled with groans and half-hearted protests, greeted his words.

"You've all got your strings of horses, and you're gonna work them real hard. If you find 'em gettin' too worn out on the trail, you can use some o' the horses you're bringin' back: but remember, we can't sell 'em to the Army if they get worn out too. Pick a different horse every day, and never ride the same one for two days runnin'. Keep them in good condition. That also means you can't drive them hard or fast. The grazin' won't be good in winter, so let 'em travel slowly enough to eat what there is. Don't try to make more than twenty miles a day.

"The team leaders will have enough money to pay for what you need in the way of supplies, and to pay for the hosses. Team leaders, there's one new thing. If the sellers want payment in gold, I'll pay at most six dollars per horse. If they want more, it'll be in greenbacks, not gold.

"*Bandidos* may try to steal some of the horses. If they do, stop 'em any way you have to. If any get killed, bury 'em deep, then drive the hoss herd over the graves so no-one can tell where they lie. We picked up some Winchester rifles from *Comancheros* on the way south. If you don't have one, see your team leaders, and we'll see how far these go around. If there ain't enough, look for more from anyone who attacks you. I reckon some of them will have 'em.

"If you fight *bandidos,* don't bother reportin' that to local lawmen, 'cause there probably won't be any! Only exception to that is the *Guardia Rural,* the Mexican federal police. They patrol nearer the border, and in areas where *bandidos* are thick on the ground. They're hard men, and they don't play games, so be straight with them. Pablo's told 'em we'll be comin', and I'll be givin' the team leaders letters confirming that you're all with me, so that should help to sort out any problems."

Pablo stepped forward. *"Amigos,* listen to *señor* Ames," he warned sternly. "The *Guardia* has a custom called *ley fuga,* the 'law of flight'. It means that someone might be shot while trying to escape, even if he was not. It saves the time, trouble and cost of taking prisoners to a court for trial, you understand?" Heads nodded. "Do not try to fool the *Guardia,* treat them with respect, and do not try to bribe them. If you try to push them around, they will treat you the same way they treat *bandidos."*

Walt nodded. "For the same reason, make *darned* sure you get a signed bill of sale for every hoss before you head for El Paso. Also, put my brand on every animal you buy, right away. If the *Guardia* stop you, they'll want proof you bought them all legally. You *don't* want them to think you're hoss thieves. Ain't no future in that!" Another loud rumble of agreement.

"All right. We'll head out in three days from now. You got that long to go over your gear, buy anything you need, an' get ready. If any of you need an advance on your wages, see me tonight. Make sure your hosses are in good condition, and feed 'em plenty of oats an' bran to build 'em up. Have them re-shod at the black-smith in town if you need to. We've got a lot o' miles to cover before we meet again."

Walt took the team leaders into the house for a private meet-ing, to make sure they knew what he expected of them. They discussed the division of the men into teams, and assigned a group to each leader, making sure that the Navajo scouts, Walt's ranch hands, Vicente's *mesteñeros,* the cowboys from northern

Texas, and the Mexican vaqueros were evenly divided. Walt handed out sheets of paper listing the Army's criteria for its horses, and warned the leaders to reject any animal that did not meet or exceed them.

"There's two branding irons per team," he said, pointing at them in a corner of the room. "My ranch brand is Rafter A. Brand each horse on the same day you buy it, and make sure to cancel any older brands by puttin' a diagonal line through 'em with a running iron. One more thing. I want good breeding stock for my ranch; mostly mares, but a few stallions too. No geldings, o' course!" The men laughed. "If you see a real good hoss, one that's well above the average, I want you to lightly underline the Rafter A brand – *lightly,* meanin' singe the hair off, not burn the skin – with a running iron. That'll tell Pablo that he shouldn't sell it to the Army, but keep it for me. I don't expect you'll find more than one horse in twenty that good, but I won't complain if you do." Laughter. "Pablo will choose others that catch his eye as they pass through here. The hair'll grow out in a few months, leavin' just the Rafter A brand behind."

IT WAS cold and clear on the morning of their departure. Pablo and two of his *vaqueros* stood by the farmhouse, sipping hot coffee, as their compatriots mounted, settled themselves in the saddle, and prepared to move out.

Walt shook Pablo's hand. "I've left plenty of money, gold and greenbacks, on deposit at Fort Bliss with the commanding officer. He knows you have the right to draw anything you need. As soon as the Army's accepted each group o' hosses, the commanding officer will give you a U.S. Government draft for them, which you can deposit with the Wells Fargo agent until I get back. We'll take all the drafts back to Fort Union and cash 'em there. Make sure the draft is for payment in gold dollars, not greenbacks – that's part o' the deal I made with the Army buyer at Fort Union."

"I will, *señor.*"

"All right, *amigo.* I'll see you in three or four months."

"Stay safe, *señor* Ames."

"I'll surely give that a whirl, Pablo."

Walt swung into the saddle, and turned to face the men. "Everyone ready?" A chorus of "No!", "Hell, no!" and "You gotta be kiddin'!" came back, and he laughed.

"All right. Teams for central and western Mexico, off you go. Good luck to you!"

More than three-quarters of the riders moved out, taking with them two extra horses per man plus twenty pack horses. They raised a cloud of dust as they turned towards the bridge over the Rio Grande between El Paso and Paso del Norte, gateway to the south.

Walt waited until the road was clear and the dust had begun to settle, then turned to the men accompanying him to Fort Clark. "Ready? Then let's ride!"

6

Twenty-two days after leaving El Paso, Walt led his men into Fort Clark. They looked around curiously as they rode their horses towards the administration building. The fort had no perimeter wall. It was a cluster of buildings around an enormous parade ground, offering enough space for an entire regiment of cavalry and its supporting units to assemble.

Walt left his men outside while he went to find the adjutant. He reported his arrival, and added, "Fort Union said they'd wire Colonel Mackenzie and ask whether there was a barracks available for us for a few days, since we're goin' into Mexico on Army business."

"Yes, we got their message," the adjutant, a young-looking lieutenant, replied. "How many men did you bring, and what sort? Cowhands? Scouts?"

"It's a mixed group; ranch hands, some white, some black and some Mexican, and a few Navajo Indian scouts. We're meetin' more cowhands from Gainesville, who'll join us here at the beginning of next month."

The lieutenant pursed his lips. "You'll have to keep your men in hand. We've got white and black soldiers here, plus a company of Seminole scouts. We've had some trouble between the different groups before. Colonel Mackenzie cracked down real hard on that, and he won't stand for any more."

"I'll make sure my men understand that," Walt promised. "They're all pretty tired. We rode all the way from Colorado to El Paso, then across southern Texas to get here. We'll spend most of our time catchin' up on sleep, I promise you!"

"Did you pass through the Texas Panhandle or the Staked Plains?"

"We went to Fort Union first, in New Mexico, then cut across the Panhandle to join the Comanche Trail. We followed it south, past the Palo Duro Canyon, then through the *Llano Estacado* to Horsehead Crossing on the Pecos River. We were checking the grazing conditions for our return trip. At the Crossing, we turned west to El Paso."

"Did you see any sign of Indians?"

"A few tracks of unshod ponies here an' there, but nothin' to speak of. We ran into some *Comancheros,* though. They were fixin' to trade rotgut whiskey an' guns to Injuns."

"Did they make trouble for you?"

"No, we made trouble for them. Killed 'em all, destroyed their whiskey, an' took their guns."

"Colonel Mackenzie will want to hear about that. He's busy right now, but can you be back here at two this afternoon?"

"Sure, if you'll let me settle my men in their barracks first, and show us where to put our horses."

"Of course. Come with me."

The barracks was a long, cold, cheerless stone building, with twenty beds set along each wall, no more than bare planks on an iron frame. They had no mattresses, sheets or blankets, but Walt assured the adjutant that his men would use their bedrolls. The adjutant promised, "I'll tell the quartermaster sergeant to bring mattresses, and fuel for the stoves, too."

The two big cast-iron stoves at either end of the barracks were soon glowing red, and his men warmed themselves over their heat with grateful sighs. The quartermaster sergeant hadn't provided enough fuel to keep them that way, so Walt had a word with him. Money changed hands, leading to a sudden and dramatic increase in the fuel supply, enough to keep the stoves burning twenty-four hours a day. Walt moved his gear into one of the tiny rooms intended for a corporal or sergeant, then left the men to relax while he returned to the administration building.

Colonel Ranald Mackenzie was younger than Walt had expected. He looked to be in his mid-thirties. He was an imposing officer, with a strong command presence that made Walt instinctively stiffen to a brace as he was introduced. The Colonel noticed at once. "Were you in the Army, Mr. Ames?" he asked as they shook hands.

"Yes, sir, but not yours," Walt replied with a half-smile. "I wore gray during the War."

"What outfit?"

"I started in the Second Tennessee Cavalry, and transferred to the First Virginia after I was sent there with an urgent message. Finished out the war with them. I was a scout and courier, sir."

"What rank?"

"Sergeant, sir."

"I see. I daresay that background has helped you out west. Scouting is a challenge anywhere, but a good scout in one region can soon learn to be a good scout in another."

"Yes, sir. That's been my experience, anyway."

"Your reputation precedes you, of course. That shot you took at Hunting Wolf in 1866 has become something of a legend. You blew his medicine bundle clean out of his hands at half a mile, if the stories are true."

"Ah... not exactly, sir. It was more like five hundred yards, and my sights were set too high. I was aiming at his chest. I just got lucky."

Mackenzie laughed. "Well, stories grow with the telling, and you did hit it, after all – and then killed him for good measure. I understand you impressed Satank, too."

"Yes, sir. He gave me my Indian name, 'Brings The Lightning'."

"He was a murderous savage, and I'm glad he's dead, but he was a brave leader for all that. Now, my adjutant tells me you had a run-in with some *Comancheros* on the way here. Where and when? What happened?"

Walt spent some time describing the engagement, showing the Colonel on his wall map where it had occurred. "We left their bodies where they lay," he concluded. "We took all the weapons and destroyed all the whiskey. I would've burned the rest, but that would've made smoke that might have attracted Injuns before we could get clear, so I left it there instead. I reckoned they'd loot it when they found it, but probl'ly not try to follow us."

"That was sensible. I'm glad you dealt with them so severely. *Comanchero* traders help support and sustain the Indian tribes, to our cost when we have to fight them. At least that's one batch of repeating rifles we won't have to face!"

Walt frowned. "I've never figured out why the Army still makes its soldiers use single-shot Springfield and Sharps rifles an' carbines, sir. It's like the generals in Washington are making their men fight with one hand tied behind their backs."

Mackenzie sighed. "I can't comment officially, you understand, but sometimes I long for the Civil War days, when our cavalry fielded seven-shot Spencer carbines. They were very effective. I wished we'd had them when I took the Fourth Cavalry into Mexico last year."

"You cleaned out the Indians there, didn't you, sir?"

"We put a dent in them, at least. The Kickapoo and Lipan Apaches had been raiding into southern Texas, so we had to hit back. We taught them a hard, painful lesson. I expect things will be more peaceful for a few years, until they forget that – then we'll have to do it all over again. My main worry right now is northern and western Texas. Things are building up to a head there. Buffalo hunters are ignoring the boundaries set in the Medicine Lodge Treaty of 1867, and shooting them on Indian land. The Kiowa and Comanche won't stand for that. The increase in settlers moving into the area is another factor. They're only on the fringes as yet, but the Indians regard that as an invasion of their traditional hunting grounds."

"Reckon if I was in their shoes, I might, too. You think they're painting for war, Colonel?"

"I think they are. I'm putting a great deal of hope in you to help us prepare for that by making up our shortfall in cavalry horses. I can't send official Army buyers into Mexico, but if you can act on our behalf and get us the quality and quantity of remounts we need, you'll have made a major contribution in your own right to our future campaigns."

"I'll surely do my best for you, Colonel. Fort Union said the Army needed up to two thousand remounts across Texas and New Mexico."

"I think that's an underestimate. If you can bring back more, I'll take them all."

"But, sir, what about payment? Fort Union told me there's only enough in the budget for that many animals."

"I see. Well, Mr. Ames, while you head into Mexico, I'm going to send an urgent message to General Sheridan. If anyone can shake loose more money for horses, he can; and he understands the needs of the cavalry from personal experience. By the time you get back, I should have word from him. I daresay it'll be positive. I'm going to ask you to put your trust in me, and in him, and bring back as many horses as you can, in that expectation."

Walt thought for a moment. "I guess I can take a chance on that, sir. If you don't buy them, I'll be able to sell them in San Antonio, although not at prices as good as the Army's payin'. I reckon I won't lose on the deal, at least. I've just got to figure out how to make my money stretch far enough to buy as many as I can, before you pay for them. That ain't gonna be easy."

"I know you'll do your best. Thank you, Mr. Ames."

Walt hesitated. "Ah... Sir, in your dealings with the Kiowa, did you ever hear of a young warrior named Laughing Raven?"

Mackenzie looked at him curiously. "As a matter of fact, I have. He's one of their sub-chiefs now, a man of some influence, and a respected warrior – one of their Dog Soldiers, in fact. Do you know him?"

"In a way, sir." Walt explained how he'd encountered the then-youth during his trip across Kansas in 1866, and how he'd given him his grandfather's rifle sleeve, reckoned to be big medicine by the Kiowa. "He gave me his tomahawk in exchange. We parted as friends. I've often wondered how he was doin'."

"He appears to be doing well. Interesting that you should have such a connection with him. Speaking of Indians, I'm told you have Navajo scouts with you. Was that authorized?"

"Yes, sir. I have a letter from the reservation agent giving them permission to work for me."

"Very good. How are they working out?"

"Real well, Colonel, but then I expected that to begin with. I got to know them in New Mexico a year or two back. Nastas, their boss, became a friend, and one of my men married his daughter – Isom Fisher, who used to be a sergeant at Fort Davis. They live with him now on Isom's spread in New Mexico, near the Navajo reservation."

"Fort Davis? So he was a buffalo soldier?"

"Yes, sir, Ninth Cavalry. He lost a hand in combat, and had to leave the service."

"That's a great pity. We lose too many good, experienced men like that, but Army regulations won't allow us to keep them on unless they're fully able-bodied. You're satisfied with the Navajos' performance, then?"

"Yes, sir. They kept us pretty well covered during the journey

south, and helped us locate, then raid those *Comancheros*. O'
course, they're helping the Army in New Mexico already. Major
Price signed up fifty of 'em at Fort Wingate last year, and I heard
he plans to do the same this year."

"He does. Based on what I've heard from both of you, I may
look to use them myself later this year. Do you think any of yours
would take on with the Cavalry for a campaign?"

"I reckon so, Colonel, if it's a short 'un. I expect to have them
back in Colorado by sometime in May. They'll spend much of the
summer with me there, breaking horses to the saddle and sorting
out breeding stock. If you need them, I can send them to any fort
or rendezvous you choose. They'll need to be back home by
winter, though."

"Do they speak English?"

"Most speak some Spanish, sir. Some can understand a little
English, but not much."

"Do you have someone who could ride with them, to be their
interpreter when dealing with the Army? A sort of civilian chief
scout?"

"Ah... if need be, I maybe could do that, Colonel. I was a
cavalry scout and courier myself, after all, so I know the sort of
work they'll be called upon to do."

"That would be very helpful. What's more, if we should
happen to run into Laughing Raven again, your connection to
him might prove useful. As a former Confederate, you won't
object to serving with the Army?"

"I reckon not, sir. Right after the War, I felt different; but
time's passed, and it's healed those wounds. I reckon you were
doin' your best for what you believed in, just as we were. We lost,
and there's no point in arguin' about that. I've built a new life for
myself since then. It's not as if I'd be wearin' your uniform,
anyway, is it, sir? I'd be a civilian scout, not a soldier."

"That's true. I'm afraid, with your injured hand, we couldn't
swear you into the ranks, for the same reason your friend

Sergeant Fisher had to be discharged. Very well, Mr. Ames. Please leave your address with my adjutant. If I have need of the Navajos, I'll telegraph, asking you to bring them to a rendezvous I'll designate."

"Will do, sir."

As he walked back to the barracks, Walt decided to ask Nastas, Gaagii and Notah, the three Navajo who'd accompanied his party, to talk to the Seminole scouts at the fort. They'd ridden with Colonel Mackenzie on the punitive expedition into Mexico last year, and would be able to advise what to expect from the Indians there. It would be a worthwhile precaution.

TO WALT'S PLEASURE, Tyler Reese arrived the following day, bringing ten cowhands with him from his ranch near Gainesville, in north central Texas. They shook hands enthusiastically.

"You're lookin' lean, mean an' tough," Tyler greeted him with a grin. "I'd kinda figured you'd run to fat after so many peaceful years out west, but all those miles from Colorado have worked it clean off of you."

"*Fat?* Huh! You're the one who ought to be fat, eatin' all that beef on the way to the railhead every year. I'm surprised you ain't sproutin' longhorns of your own!"

"Naw. My head's too hard for them. They can't get out through my skull. Did Jess Manning make it safely to El Paso?"

"He sure did. He's on his way into Mexico now, with close on fifty of my men and yours. They're goin' to be workin' hard over there, while we do the same down here."

"Glad to hear it. I'm thankin' you for the chance to get in on this. A lot o' my money is tied up in cattle, but I brought three thousand to invest in hosses. If this works out like you hope, that should double my money or better. That'll help me build up my

nest egg for the ranch I want to buy in the Panhandle, soon as
they clean the Injuns outta the way."

"Have you got enough saved yet?"

"Oh, heck, no! I've got about ten thousand in cash, the same
in cattle to drive up to Kansas come the spring, plus the value o'
my land. Call it twenty-five thousand or so, all in all. That's not
near enough for the size of spread I want, or the cattle to go on it.
It's dry country up there, an' not well grassed, so you may need
ten or more acres per steer. I'm lookin' to buy at least a hundred
thousand acres, more if I can afford it."

Walt whistled in surprise. "You ain't thinkin' small, are you?"

"Nope. If I get in early, as soon as it's safe, I can buy land right
off the surveyors' plats as they draw 'em. I'll go for the well-
watered places, to lock up the land around them. Grazin'
without water is useless, so I can buy that cheap later, if I get the
water rights first. Thing is, there's others with the same idea. I'll
have to have enough money right from the get-go to buy what I
need. If I have to wait, all the good land will be gone, and it'll
cost a lot more. Trouble is, Texas is still messed up from Recon-
struction. Governor Davis made sure former Rebs like you and I
found it hard to get bank loans an' the like. Meanwhile, his
cronies got anything they wanted. He's just been voted out, but
he's tryin' to hold on to office any way he can. The courts have
weighed in, and they say he's even asked President Grant to send
troops."

Walt frowned. "I can't see the Yankees doing that. It'd start
another civil war!"

"I hope you're right. We need Davis gone, so Texas can get to
growin' again."

"Good luck with that, and with your ranch huntin'. When the
time comes to buy it, talk to me. I may have money to invest in a
ranch, for a few years at least. I reckon we trust each other
enough to make it work, in a way that's fair to both of us; and if
I'm a partner, you won't have to pay interest to a bank."

Tyler's face lit up. "Thanks, Walt. That may make all the difference. When the time comes, you'll hear from me for sure."

Walt gave everybody two days to relax, and to rest their horses. He bought more supplies from the Fort's sutler for the journey south, noting in passing that his stocks were limited. He'd have to make other arrangements for the return journey.

The Navajo scouts visited the Seminoles, and came back with interesting news. The local scouts reckoned there was still a risk of Indian attack just over the border in the region of San Felipe del Rio, which the Americans called simply 'Del Rio'. They suggested that instead of crossing there, Walt should take his party further south to Eagle Pass, and cross the Rio Grande there to the Mexican town of Piedras Negras, returning the same way with his horse herds. Walt changed his plans accordingly.

Walt took the opportunity to sound out his Navajo scouts about the possibility of working with the Army if hostilities with the Comanche and Kiowa recommenced later that year. To a man, they were enthusiastic. Nastas said with approval, "It will let the boys grow into men. By the time this horse-buying journey is over, they will have learned a lot and matured even more. They will then be able to work with the rest of us as scouts in their own right."

"What about their families?" Walt asked. "Won't we have to get their permission?"

"No. If I say it is in order, that is all that will be needed."

"We'd better have all o' you head for your homes after this trip, to visit your families before you come back to the ranch. That way, if you're gone for longer than planned, they'll know about it, an' you can leave your new hosses safely with them. O' course, this may not come to anything. We'll have to see what happens."

Nastas nodded. "That will also give those who wish it, the chance to remain at home. I can get others to take their place. There are many young men eager to ride the war trail. They cannot do so on the reservation, but to serve as Army scouts, they will be given permission to leave it."

"As long as they're as good as you all are, I'm happy with that. I'll ask the Colonel to give me a letter sayin' what he wants, so the Reservation Agent will understand."

Walt couldn't help smiling at the eager expression on young Notah's face. It showed his aspirations very clearly.

That evening Pablo's four men arrived, tired, but grateful to be able to rest for a brief period before heading south with the group once more. They brought good news. They'd arranged horse fairs at Saltillo and Monterrey, in the heart of horse-breeding country, and expected ranchers to bring their herds from a hundred miles or more around each town.

"I think they may bring far more horses than you need, *señor,*" Carlos, the leader of Pablo's group, warned Walt. "You may have to send many away."

"Maybe not, if their prices are low enough," Walt replied thoughtfully, remembering Colonel Mackenzie's wishes. "Up at El Paso, we were told that if we pay in gold, we might get good hosses for as little as six dollars a head. D'you think that's true here too?"

"Possibly, *señor,* especially if the alternative is to trail their horses all the way back to their homes. It is a low price, but gold is something a man can touch and feel. It will be more acceptable than banknotes. For the best horses, you might have to pay a little more, perhaps seven or eight dollars."

"We'll have to see about that. All right, rest and relax tomorrow. If you need anything from the sutler's store, let me know and I'll buy it for you. We ride south the day after tomorrow."

7

Walt looked at the rickety wooden bridge across the Rio Grande with some trepidation. "What d'you think, Tyler?" he asked. "Will that thing take the weight of all of us, and our remuda, at the same time?"

"I wouldn't like to chance it. What with our ridin' hosses, remounts and pack hosses, we've got close to a hundred head. I'd take 'em across in two groups, was I you, and in single file."

"That's what we'll do, then. You split the men and horses behind me. I'll go across with the first half, to smooth things over on the Mexican side. You follow along with the rest once we're across."

"I'll do that. Reckon when we come back, we'd best drive our hoss herd through the old ford, rather than trust 'em to this bridge."

"Good idea, if the river's low enough. Let's remember that."

The Mexican authorities had been informed of the group's arrival, and the reason for their visit, so there were no problems in getting everyone into the country, even the Navajo scouts. The only worry was when Walt had to declare how much money he was bringing with him. The official's eyebrows flew up when he heard the sum of ten thousand dollars, but he relaxed when he was informed that it was to buy horses. Nevertheless, the rest of the border officials looked distinctly covetous. Walt wished he hadn't had to mention the amount he was carrying, but there was nothing for it.

As they rode away from the crossing, he muttered to Tyler, "I didn't like the way the officials looked when they heard about my money."

"Neither did I. I'm glad they didn't ask me about mine. Reckon some of 'em might try to fine us for something, or figure out another way to get their hands on it?"

"Maybe. I reckon they might tell local *bandidos* about it in return for a cut of the loot. We'd best keep our eyes open."

Sure enough, before they'd gone a dozen miles, one of the rear guard rode forward. "Boss, there's a couple o' men on horseback followin' us. They ain't comin' any closer, just hangin' back about a mile or two. Thing is, when we go over a hill, they close up, like they was hurryin' to make sure we didn't turn off somewhere. Soon as they crest the hill and can see us again, they slow down and keep their distance."

"Followin' us for sure," Tyler said with a black scowl. "Want me to take some o' my men back there an' deal with them?"

Walt shook his head. "Followin' us ain't a crime. If you try to stop them, and they show fight, what're you gonna tell the *Guardia Rural?* We'd have no legal reason to shoot 'em. Naw, we'll just double our guard at night, an' keep on the alert. If they want to jump a party this strong an' this well armed, they're gonna have to work for it."

The two watchers kept their distance throughout the day. As the group turned into a field about fifteen miles from Piedras Negras, to bed down for the night, they halted for a while, watching the activities, then turned and rode back in the direction from which they had come.

"They're goin' somewhere to report to someone," Walt

guessed as he watched them through his spyglass. "I'm willin' to bet they, or two more, will be back tomorrow mornin', to see where we're goin'."

"No, thanks," Tyler retorted with a grin. "I only bet on sure things for me, not for the other guy!"

Over the next few days, Walt's prediction was proved correct. Every morning, as the sun rose, two observers – not always the same two – were waiting on a rise about a mile away. They followed the group during the day, and watched while they made camp in the evenings; then they turned and rode away.

Late in the afternoon of their fourth day in Mexico, they reached the small town of Nueva Rosita. There appeared to be some sort of festival in progress; a small band was playing, stalls had been set up in and around the main square, and vendors were doing a brisk trade selling food and drink. Walt was conscious of the eager eyes of his men on the goings-on, and made a snap decision.

"Boys, we'll make camp for the night on the far side of town. I want four men on watch at all times. The first four will guard the camp an' the hosses while the rest come back here to have some fun. I'll make sure they're relieved by seven, to let them do the same. Don't flash your money around, and don't bully or shove your way through the crowds. Remember, this ain't our country – it's theirs, and we want 'em to sell us their hosses. Treat 'em the way we'd like our guests to treat us."

The horses were watered at a nearby stream, then picketed in a field to prevent them straying. Their saddles and pack saddles were piled in the campsite. Walt warned everyone, with a grin, "Put your bedrolls out ready before you go into town. You may find it tricky when you come back later tonight, if you've been celebratin' too hard!" With laughter and quips flying back and forth, the men complied.

Walt had a word with the first four guards, and those he'd delegated to relieve them later, before walking back to town.

"Keep your eyes open and don't slack off. Remember, we've had those men watchin' us ever since we crossed the border. I'd not put it past them to try somethin' tonight, while we're all sleepin' off the fun. Don't let them get past you because you're day-dreamin' about the fun you're gonna have, or did have, in town."

"Got it, boss." "I hear ya, boss." The four rumbled their agreement, and kept their rifles in their hands as they watched the surrounding countryside.

Satisfied, Walt followed most of his men back into town. It was only a couple of hundred yards to the main square, so they didn't bother to take their horses. The men split up into small groups and wandered around, buying food from this stall, a drink from that, and eyeing the attractive Mexican girls with appreciation.

Walt drew laughter from onlookers when he stopped at a stall selling straw products – baskets, hats and the like. He took off his Stetson hat, laid it on the table, and picked up a *sombrero* with an enormous brim, almost a yard wide. The children in particular seemed to find that very funny, giggling at this strange *gringo* trying on one of their hats, trying to look like one of their people. They couldn't help staring at the metal hook on his left wrist. He bent down to their level and wriggled it back and forth, drawing shrieks of merriment from the little boys and smiles from their parents as they scrambled back to get away from it.

As he straightened up, an unkempt, unshaven man wearing greasy, dirty clothing stepped in front of him and picked up his Stetson from the table. *"Esto es mio ahora,"* he said with a smile that didn't reach his eyes. "This is mine now."

Walt was sure he'd seen this man through his spyglass. He'd been one of those following them over the past few days. Three more men shouldered their way through the crowd to stand in a half-circle behind him. The locals fell silent, edging away to make space around them.

"No, it's not. It's mine," Walt told him as he took off the sombrero and set it down on the table.

"I didn't ask you," the man replied with a cold grin. "If I want something, I take it."

"You're not taking that one. I'll tell you just once, politely, to put it down."

"Why don't you make me, *cabron?*" He tossed the hat behind him as he bent forward, hand hovering menacingly over the knife on his hip. A little girl operating the stall next door, selling what looked like lemonade or something similar, let out a cry of anguish as the flying hat knocked her big glass jug off the table. It shattered as it hit the hard ground, broken glass and liquid flying in all directions.

Behind the speaker, the other three men tensed for action. Walt realized at once what they were trying to do. The border officials had seen that he, as leader, was carrying the group's money. If anything happened to him, these men – or those who had sent them – probably reckoned that the rest of the group would be easier to deal with.

Without warning, or telegraphing his movements by getting into a better position, he launched a forward stamping kick that smacked into the kneecap of the man facing him, hard enough that his knee joint reversed itself with a sickening *crack!* The man screamed in sudden anguish and toppled sideways, his hands going to his injured leg as he writhed in agony on the ground. Behind him, the other men's hands stabbed towards their holsters – only to come to a frozen halt as Walt's right hand made a sight-defying flip, and his revolver lined rock-solid on them.

There was a sudden, deafening silence around the stall, spreading out into the square. Only the sobs of the girl behind the next table and the moans of the injured man could be heard.

Walt said slowly, softly, "Do you want to live, or do you want to die?"

Their mouths still agape, for a moment none of the three could answer. At last one said, shakily, "L-live, *señor.*"

"Then shed your guns, very slowly, very carefully. Use one finger and thumb only. Let them fall at your feet. Your knives, too."

A couple of Walt's men had seen the trouble, and arrived on the run, guns drawn. "You need help, boss?" one asked.

"Stick around. When they've dropped their guns and knives, search them to make sure they haven't got any more. One of you disarm that man on the ground, then search him too. Check inside their belts, boots and hats as well." He half-smiled, thinking of the Remington Double Derringer hideout guns he carried inside the crown of his hat and his left boot top. If he found them useful, others might too.

Within two minutes, all four men had been disarmed and searched. Walt holstered his gun, then piled their weapons on the table beside him. He looked around. "Where is the *alcalde?*"

An older man pushed through the crowd. "I am the mayor, *señor.*"

"Do you know these men?"

"I have never seen them before, *señor.*"

"All right. Is there an officer of the law in town?"

"No, *señor.* We have little crime here. We are too small. A patrol of the *Guardia Rural* visits from time to time."

"Very well. Please take charge of their guns and knives."

"*Si, señor.*"

"Also, please ask those who saw what just happened to give a statement about it. They need not lie, or say much: only what they saw. Please give them to me when they are ready. I will hand them in to the *Guardia Rural* in Monclova, along with my own statement, so they can investigate if they wish."

The alcalde smiled for the first time. "I shall, *señor.* Thank you for doing that. It will avoid trouble for us. I shall add my own statement also, and write them for those who cannot do so." He called out two men and told them to run to his office, taking the guns and knives with them, and come back with paper and pencils to take the statements.

Walt turned to the three men who'd sided with the trouble-maker. "Your friend broke that girl's jug. You're going to help him buy her a new one." To his own men, he added, "Get every cent they've got, and give it to me."

The three men stiffened, outraged, as their pockets were emptied and all their money taken. Walt did the same to the moaning man on the ground. He counted swiftly. He wasn't familiar with all the coins in his hand, but it looked like the total would come to the equivalent of a few dollars.

"Watch them," he told his men, then walked over to the still-weeping girl. "*Niña,* I'm sorry these men broke your jug. This will help you buy a new one." He laid the money on the table, and her crying suddenly stilled as she stared at it with big eyes. He fumbled in his pocket, and laid a five-dollar half-eagle on top of the pile. There was a hiss of indrawn breath from the onlookers, swiftly stilled as Walt looked around. They clearly recognized the gold coin, and were in no doubt as to its value. It was probably more than she'd have made from selling her lemonade, or what-ever it was, at two or three of these *fiestas.*

He picked up his hat from the ground, and dusted it off as he asked, "Does this girl have any family here?"

An old man stepped forward. "I am her *abuelo, señor.* Her name is Maria. I am Guillermo."

"Her grandfather, eh? I'm glad to meet you, *señor.* My name is Walter Ames. If you'll please wait with Maria for a moment, I'll get rid of these men, then come back to see both of you safely home. I wouldn't want anyone to get ideas about taking that money for themselves."

"I will, *señor.* Thank you."

Walt put on his hat, then turned back to the three disarmed and penniless men. "Pick up your friend, and carry him to where you left your horses. We'll be behind you." He indicated his own men. "Don't do anything stupid."

They followed the four men to where their horses were tied to a hitching rail. Walt halted them before they got there, and had his men unload the rifles in the horses' saddle boots and remove all the ammunition from their saddlebags. When he was satisfied, he told the three, "All right, put your friend on his horse, then get astride your own and get out of here. Don't come back. If you do, it won't end so well for you."

One of the four looked down at him from his saddle, his eyes ugly. "We will not forget this, *señor* – or you."

"See that you don't. Remember how it ended, too, and don't get any ideas. You'll live longer that way."

The men reined their horses around, two of them supporting the injured man in his saddle, and trotted away, heading northeast out of town.

Walt and his ranch hands watched them go until they were half a mile away, then turned back to the plaza. They didn't see the four men meet up with two more, who rode out of the bushes a mile out of town. The six men halted in the road as they held a brief conversation, then turned off the track into the bushes.

Back at the plaza, the old man and his granddaughter were waiting at the table when Walt returned. He smiled at him. *"Con su permiso,* shall we see your granddaughter safely home?"

"Thank you, *señor."*

The two lived just a few blocks away, in a run-down adobe shack on the edge of town. It had a small vegetable patch behind it, and a donkey in a little fenced enclosure next to it. As they approached, Maria scampered ahead, clutching her new-found wealth in her hand as she called excitedly, *"Mamacita!* See what the nice man gave me!"

A tired-looking woman stepped out of the door. She looked to be in her late twenties or early thirties, but already her face bore lines of care and concern. Her eyes widened in surprise as her daughter thrust the money into her hands. "What is this? Where did it come from?"

The *abuelo* raised his voice. "Do not worry, Edelmira. Some bad *hombres* broke her jug. This *gringo* stopped them, and made them pay for it, and gave her the gold coin besides. He has just walked us home."

"That's how it was, *señora*," Walt confirmed, doffing his hat to her. "I wanted to make sure no-one else gave her any trouble."

"Th-thank you, *señor!*"

"*Si, muchas gracias, señor!*" young Maria piped up, beaming.

"I have nothing but water, *señor,* but if you would like some...?" her mother asked.

"Thank you. That would be very kind of you."

"Please, come in and sit down." She ushered him ceremoniously through the door into the small room within. It was lit by the fading daylight, and by an oil lamp on a small table against one wall, already lit.

Walt glanced around as he sat down on a rickety chair at the table. His eyes fell on a faded gray kepi hanging from the wall above the fireplace. He stiffened as he noticed its badge. Glancing at the *abuelo* as he also sat down, he asked, "Is that a Confederate hat – one that the soldiers in gray wore during the big Anglo war, some years ago?"

"*Si, señor.* It is. It came from a wounded man whom I found in the mountains over there. He died before I could bring him to safety. I brought his hat and some other things here, to keep them safe, as he asked me."

"May I look at it, please? I wore one like it during that war."

"Of course, *señor.*"

Walt rose, took down the hat, and inspected it closely. It was a standard medium gray uniform kepi, dusty, but still in good condition. Three rows of gold braid were sewn onto the top, sides, front and back of the kepi to indicate field officer's rank, and three rows of braid ran around the hat above a yellow band that marked the wearer as a cavalry officer. The peak was of black leather, and brass buttons marked 'C.S.A.' secured the band.

The old man watched him closely. "You said you wore that uniform too, *señor?*"

"Yes, I did."

"Then it may be the providence of God that you came to our aid this day. You see, the man who wore that gave me some things. He made me promise that I would give them to his comrades in arms when they came looking for him – but none ever did. I have kept them to this day, waiting for their arrival."

Walt sat down slowly. "Well... I suppose you could call me his comrade in arms. We fought for the same side, after all. What are they?"

"I will fetch them, *señor.*"

The old man shuffled through a curtained opening into another room. Walt heard him open what sounded like the lid of a trunk, rummaging through it. In a moment, he returned holding a well-worn leather satchel. It was stamped 'C.S.A.' on the flap above the buckle.

"Here, *señor.*" The old man handed over the satchel.

Walt opened it, and took out a holstered 1860 Army Colt, a big knife in a leather sheath, a pocket compass, and a small, thick book. His face lit up as he saw the knife. "This is an Ames knife!" he exclaimed, drawing it from its sheath. "It was the first knife designed for the Army, way back in '49." He hefted the big, heavy, foot-long blade. It was still in fair condition, apart from a few nicks and discolorations. "They only made a thousand of them. I've only seen two before, both during the War."

He replaced it in its sheath, then drew the revolver. Its surface bore a light patina of rust, and the percussion caps on the cylinder nipples had all been fired. Walt sighed softly to himself. Clearly, the old man had not known how to clean it. By now, blackpowder salts had surely corroded the inside of the barrel and cylinders, probably too badly for further use. He re-holstered it, vowing to clean it as soon as he could, in case anything could be salvaged.

The pocket compass proved to be a high-quality instrument, made in London, England by James Parkes and Son, and dated 1850. Its face, almost two inches in diameter, showed all thirty-two major and minor points of the compass rose. The needle swung straight to North and remained steady on the bearing when he opened the compass cover and held it level. Walt nodded in approval as he closed its cover.

"What is the book, *señor?*" he asked as he picked it up.

"I do not know. None of us can read. I have kept it unopened since the day he gave it to me."

Walt opened it. The handwritten inscription on the first page read, "Diary of Captain Gilbert d'Assaily, Confederate States Army, of Baton Rouge in Louisiana, begun on January 1, 1865, in continuation of his four previous wartime diaries."

Fascinated, Walt flipped through the first few pages. The Captain had been serving on the staff of General Beauregard in North Carolina as the diary opened. He described the heartbreak of repeated, unsuccessful efforts to halt General Sherman's northward advance towards Virginia. Walt had to tear himself away from the text, to look up at the old man.

"Yes, he was my comrade in arms. We were in different units, but we served the same cause. Where did you find him?"

"A day's ride from here, just before you reach Santa Rosa de Múzquiz, on the left-hand side of the road, you will see a valley reaching into the mountains. There is a narrow trail leading into it from the road. If you follow it for about five miles, it enters a horseshoe canyon. The trail winds up one side, turns at the bend, then continues up the other side to come out on top. From there, it goes on through the mountains, with more trails leading off it.

"I was climbing the horseshoe trail when I found him. He had been coming down from the other direction. He had been shot several times, and had fallen off his horse. It had stayed by him, but galloped off when I tried to catch it. I never saw it again. He spoke some Spanish. We talked for a little while, until he died. I buried him in the horseshoe bend, at the side of the road, and rolled a rock over his grave. I carved a cross on it."

He sighed. "When I came back that way a week later, someone had rolled the rock off his grave and dug up his body. He had been searched – his clothes were disarranged."

"Was he wearing uniform?"

"A mixture of uniform and civilian clothes, *señor*. Whoever searched him left his body exposed. I re-buried him, and rolled the rock back over his grave. Since then, as far as I know, his rest has not been disturbed."

"You don't know where he was coming from?"

"He did not tell me, *señor*. He asked me to give these things to his comrades in arms, but died before he could name them. I brought his belongings back here, but never saw or heard of his comrades. May I give them to you? It is more fitting that they be with you, who wore the same uniform as him, than with me, I think."

Walt hesitated. Should he accept them? He realized, after a moment's thought, that there was no reasonable alternative, and nodded. "I'll take them. When I've read this book, I may find out what he wanted his comrades to do with them. If not, I'll send them to his relatives, if I can find them."

"Thank you, *señor*. That will lift a burden of honor from me."

"Thank you for bearing it faithfully for all these years. If it's given to the dead to know such things, he'll know you've done what you promised you would do." Walt nodded to the hat he'd left lying on the table. "If you kept these things in your trunk, *señor*, why did you keep his hat on the wall above the fireplace?"

Edelmira said softly, "*Señor*, I asked him to do that. Every night, when we pray before going to bed, we pray a decade of the Rosary for the soul of that man, even though we never knew his name."

Walt had to swallow a sudden lump in his throat. He coughed, then said gently, "In that case, *señora,* please keep the hat there, and continue to pray for his soul. His name was Gilbert d'Assaily. If you would be so kind, please pray also for me. It would be a comfort to me, as I have had no-one else to do so since the death of my wife, two years ago."

"We shall, *señor,*" she promised. Maria and her grandfather nodded their solemn assent.

8

Walt was too preoccupied with the diary to go back to the fiesta. He returned to the camp site, sat down by the fire, lit a lantern, and started to read.

Captain d'Assaily described General Beauregard's efforts to stem the Sherman-led Union tide rushing up through the Carolinas. Without adequate resources, Beauregard had failed at every step, leading to the crushing news in late February 1865 that he had been relieved of his command and replaced by General Johnston. For the remainder of the war, Beauregard had served Johnston loyally, but was never again given a combat command. Instead, he had been shunted off to administrative duties, which he performed without open complaint. However, he had confided his bitter disappointment to his aide, and d'Assaily had faithfully recorded it.

After Lee's surrender at Appomattox, Johnston and Beauregard had traveled to meet with Confederate President Jefferson Davis on April 13, 1865. Captain d'Assaily had accompanied his general. He was not present at the meeting, but wrote that both Generals had told the President it would be necessary to make surrender overtures to General Sherman, as further resistance was pointless.

"After the meeting, as they were leaving," the Captain wrote, "the President asked General Beauregard whether he could spare a courageous, intelligent officer, whose loyalty to the cause of the Confederacy was beyond question, for a secret mission of the highest importance. General Beauregard immediately turned to me, and introduced me to the President as entirely meeting his requirements. I was forthwith ordered to accompany President Davis. I bade General Beauregard farewell, not knowing whether we should ever meet again. It was an emotional parting for both of us."

Walt read on with growing excitement as the Captain described being taken to a railway goods wagon, part of a special train from Richmond. He was passed through the sentries around it by the President. It was mostly empty, except for a few boxes, sacks, satchels and saddlebags filled with gold coins and paper currency, both Union and Confederate – the remaining contents of the Confederate Treasury. They had been spirited out of Richmond barely hours before the capital city's surrender to Union forces on April 2.

President Davis advised Captain d'Assaily that some Confederate forces in Texas were determined to fight on. He could not give them any further material support except to send part of the treasury to them, so they could buy what they needed locally. He asked the Captain to smuggle $35,000 in U.S. pre-war gold double-eagles through Union lines, then get them to Brigadier-General Joseph Shelby and his forces, along with a personal message from the President. He did not know Shelby's present location, so the Captain would have to use his initiative to locate him and deliver the gold.

Walt swore under his breath as he mentally calculated. $35,000 in double-eagles... there would be one thousand, seven hundred and fifty coins in that sum... one double-eagle weighed just under one and a fifth ounces... so the total weight of the money would be about one hundred and thirty pounds. "Not too bad," he muttered to himself. "A single pack horse could carry that much without trouble."

That was probably the reason for the amount, he realized. One rider could manage one pack horse with relative ease. He'd done so himself, many times, during and since the Civil War. Any more money would require a second pack horse. That would make managing and concealing them more difficult when sneaking through enemy lines. The President's advisers had probably settled on one pack horse load as being the most practical amount they could send. As for gold coin, that was an obvious choice. Confederate paper currency might or might not be accepted in exchange for supplies, particularly given the imminent end of the war, but gold would be eagerly accepted by anyone, anywhere, at any time.

"I shook the President's hand and solemnly promised him, on my honor and the honor of Louisiana, my home state, that I would succeed in this mission or die trying. He promoted me to Major on the spot, taking insignia of rank from a member of his own bodyguard, and putting them on me with his own hands as a mark of his confidence and respect. I saluted him, and went to the horse cars to select two animals. I chose a black to ride and a brown to serve as pack horse, both geldings in very good condition. They had been well fed, unlike most of our mounts, thanks to belonging to the Presidential Guard. I loaded the horses, collected travel money and rations, and rode away into the night."

Walt rapidly skimmed through the following pages. The Captain – no, a Major now, he reminded himself – had made his way through the Carolinas and Georgia, moving carefully at night only, avoiding Union patrols. As news of the surrender spread, he found the going easier because Union forces largely stopped patrolling, content to celebrate their victory in their camps while they waited to go home. He had been able to hunt for food, although unable to buy rations from farmers due to the destruction left by Sherman's march to the sea.

He had reached his parents' home in Baton Rouge at the end of May, and broke his journey there for a few weeks. They were overjoyed to see him, but nonplussed by his determination to complete his last mission. Through newspaper reports, he'd learned that General Shelby had decided to cross into Mexico with his forces, rather than surrender them to the Union. He had approved wholeheartedly of this defiant attitude, even more so because he'd seen the destruction wrought by Sherman's army in a wide swath across Georgia. He was determined to offer both the gold and his services to General Shelby as soon as possible.

At this point, Walt was interrupted by the return of the relief sentries from the fiesta, and the departure of those who had stood guard to join the festivities. He poured himself some coffee from the pot on the coals, and settled down to read again.

The diary described how Major d'Assaily had bought passage on a paddlewheel riverboat to New Orleans, then a ticket on a coastal steamer to Brownsville in Texas. He had traveled in civilian clothing, concealing the gold, his uniform and his weapons in two steamer trunks, and passing himself off as a merchant. He noted in passing his deep regret that he could not take his cavalry saber with him, as it could not be carried openly without attracting unwelcome attention, but was too long to fit into the trunks. He had reached Brownsville by late July, where he'd learned that the French-imposed Emperor of Mexico, Maximilian, had offered land to General Shelby and his veterans in the vicinity of Vera Cruz. However, he was unable to obtain passage on a ship going there. He had decided to buy horses in Brownsville, cross into Mexico at Matamoros, and continue his journey overland.

He had paid a smuggler to get him and his horses across the river above the port, without going through border formalities that would reveal the gold; but the smuggler had somehow learned what he was carrying. He'd tried to kill him, and steal his horses and the pack saddle, as soon as they'd landed in Mexico. The Major had fought back, receiving a stab wound to his left arm, and had managed to recover the gold while killing the smuggler. He had headed westward towards Monterrey, away from the coast, to avoid any of the man's colleagues who might seek vengeance.

Unfortunately, the smuggler must have spread the word about the gold. Others had followed him. In two brisk fights, he'd killed two more, but, heavily outnumbered, he'd been forced to turn north, fleeing from their pursuit. He'd reached Monclova, only to find that some of them had got ahead of him and hired local assistance. In a fight outside the town, he was wounded by a bullet, and forced to head northwest towards San Buenaventura. From there, he had turned north again, heading into the foothills of the Sierra Madre Oriental.

In his last neat, easily legible entry, he wrote that he had taken to a mountain trail that climbed seemingly ever upward. "I know not where it leads, or how long it will take me to get there, or even if these fiends from hell on my trail will let me live that long," he had written despairingly. "I shall go on as far as I can, and fight as long as I can; but I am sore wounded, and do not know how much time is left to me. May God help me!"

There was a blank page after that entry. Turning it, Walt found a scribbled, half-legible entry in pencil, sometimes obscured by dark brown stains that he instantly recognized as dried human blood. He'd seen enough of it in his life to be certain of that.

"I write these words in haste," Major d'Assaily had written. "They wounded my pack horse. It could not carry its load any further. I buried the gold and President Davis' message beneath a flat, triangular rock, midway along the top of the southern wall of a canyon that lies due west of Rancherias, about seven miles from it. I could see the town clearly, and took a bearing on it. Also, I took a bearing on the church tower of a town that my map calls Santa Rosa de Múzquiz. It bore precisely north by east.

"From that place, I followed the trail to the top of the valley, where it turned north. There I removed its saddle and released the injured pack horse, to find its own way out of these mountains, if it survives. I passed two trails that joined mine, then this trail entered a horseshoe bend in a deep valley.

"My wounds have disabled me. I have fallen from my horse, and can go no further. I killed those hot on my heels, but they wounded me twice more, and others are sure to come. I write these last words in the hope that none of my pursuers can read English. God grant that my Confederate brothers in arms may find this diary, and retrieve the gold, and make good use of it for our cause. I can do no more. Farewell and Godspeed. Pray for my soul."

The last few words faded out in a dashed scribble, as if the writer could no longer see clearly or control his hand. Walt gulped, imagining the sheer determination and willpower that had driven Major d'Assaily to this last effort. He had surely kept faith with his country and his cause, no matter what the outcome of his final mission.

Walt closed the diary, poured more coffee, and sat back to think. Had the gold ever been recovered? It seemed unlikely. The old man had said that the Major's body had been dug up and searched by unknown persons, presumably those who had been pursuing him; but by then his diary had been taken to Nueva Rosita. They would not have known who had it, or where to look for it. In its absence, could they have found any sign of where the gold had been buried?

"I guess there's only one way to find out," he said softly to himself, feeling a growing sense of excitement. "I've got to go look for it myself – but I've got hosses to buy, too. Can I do both at the same time?"

He fetched his map and examined it closely by the light of the lantern, calculating distances and times. He also had to consider whom to take with him. It would be foolhardy to go into unknown country alone, particularly since he'd had evidence, earlier that night, that it was hardly free of unsavory characters. He might have to fight them, just as Major d'Assaily had done. There might also be Indians in the Sierra Madre Oriental, the mountain range forming the eastern spine of Mexico, who might regard a lone white man as easy prey. No, he had to have at least one person with him... but who?

He puzzled over the problem long into the evening. By the time the others returned from the fiesta, he had the kernel of a plan. He decided to sleep on it, and see how it looked in the morning.

Walt woke at dawn, and rolled out of his blankets. He shook Tyler and Nastas awake, then stoked up the coals of last night's fire with fresh fuel and put coffee on to brew. As soon as they were dressed, they came together by the fire.

Walt explained to them the events of the previous evening, and what he'd read in Major d'Assaily's diary, without going into detail about what he'd carried on his mission or where he'd buried it. He described it simply as "an important dispatch for General Shelby", which was true, of course, but left out a lot.

Tyler was fascinated. "Dang, what a piece of history! What are you gonna do with that diary?"

"I'll try to return it to his parents, if I can trace them. I know they lived in Baton Rouge at the end of the war. That's a starting point – but it's not why I woke you. I'd like to see if I can find what he buried."

"I sure would, too! You gonna go after it?"

"I reckon so, if you'll come with me, Nastas. I'll need someone to watch my back while I look. The people who killed the Major, all those years ago, may still be around, and they may be watching for anyone trying to find his back trail."

"I shall come," the Navajo agreed. "Just the two of us?"

"Yes, just us two. Tyler, I'll leave you in charge of the others. Take them down to Monclova. It's about four days' ride from here. If we haven't joined you by the time you get there, wait up to six days for us. We have time in our schedule before the first horse fair, so that won't delay us much, and it'll give the horses a chance to rest."

Tyler frowned. "What if you ain't there after six days?"

"Then you'll have to take the men down to Monterrey and Saltillo, and continue the mission. If we don't reach you there, something serious has gone wrong."

"I'll have some of the boys come lookin', then."

"That'd be good, but only if you can hire locals to replace them and keep on buying horses. Remember, we've got a job to do. That comes first. I shouldn't really be goin' off like this, but I gotta admit, that diary's caught my imagination. I'd kinda like to do as the Major asked, and recover his message, even if only for the sake of history."

"I can't argue with you. We both wore the same uniform, so we know how he'd have felt about his last mission. When will you leave?"

"Soon's we've eaten. You take the main body south, while Nastas and I turn east."

THE SIX MEN had moved closer to Nueva Rosita during the night. They watched from a clump of bushes less than half a mile from the camp as Walt and Tyler got the men together, explained what they were going to do, and saddled their horses.

"What's that *hijo de puta* doing?" one asked sourly, trying to make out what Walt was doing as he selected weapons and other items from his two personal pack horses, and loaded them onto another. Meanwhile, Nastas collected food, utensils and their bedrolls, and loaded them onto a second pack horse.

"It's different from what they've done other mornings," another admitted.

They watched as the group mounted. Tyler waved, then led the main body onto the trail to Monclova. Walt and Nastas watched them go, then reined their horses around and rode off in the direction of Santa Rosa de Múzquiz.

"They're splitting up!" the first speaker snapped. He looked around. "All right. Hernan, you and Onofre follow the main group today, as usual. Report back to the boss tonight, and tell him about this. Meanwhile, the rest of us will follow those two, to find out what they're up to. We may be able to get them on an isolated stretch of the trail. We owe them for last night, after all." His voice was savage.

"But I can't ride!" Tiburcio moaned. His knee was tightly wrapped in cloth torn from a shirt. "That *cabron* screwed up my leg too badly! What am I supposed to do, Esteban?"

The leader shrugged callously. "That's your problem. Sandoval wants that man dead, an' we're the only ones around to do it."

The injured man grabbed Esteban's arm. "You bastard, you can't just treat me like *mierda* to be scraped off your boot!"

Esteban's eyes narrowed. He whipped a knife from its sheath at his waist, and plunged it into Tiburcio's chest. The *bandido* opened his mouth to scream in pain, but Esteban's other hand came up to pinch his cheeks hard, forcing his mouth shut again as he worked the knife back and forth, thrusting deeper. All Tiburcio could do was let out a muffled moan of agony as he sagged, staring at his murderer in disbelief. It took him less than thirty seconds to lose consciousness, and another minute or so to bleed out internally.

Esteban wiped the knife blade clean on his victim's shirt, and sheathed it. "When you report back tonight, tell the boss he doesn't have to pay Tiburcio any more," he said to Hernan. Guffaws of coarse, merciless laughter greeted his sally. "Felix,

Hector, take the rifle ammunition he got from Hernan and Onofre last night. Divide it in three, and give me my share. That, plus what we got from them earlier, will give each of us two full reloads for our rifles. That should be more than enough to handle those two."

"What about our belt guns and knives?"

Esteban snorted. "You saw how fast that *gringo* drew last night. He's as good as the boss. We'll have no chance against him with revolvers. Much better shoot him from a safe distance with our rifles. I've got Hernan's knife. That'll be enough for a day or two. When we've dealt with those two men, we'll have their guns; and we can come back via Nueva Rosita, and get our guns from the *alcalde*."

"What if he don't want to give them to us?" Felix asked.

Esteban gave a slow, hard smile. "I hope he doesn't. He's got a pretty daughter. We'll use her to teach him the hard way not to defy us!"

9

"They are still there," Nastas reported later that afternoon. "They are hanging well back, two or three miles. There are three of them, not four."

"Maybe the one I kicked can't ride," Walt guessed, accepting the spyglass he'd loaned Nastas earlier. "Did this help?"

"Very much. It brings people closer than binoculars. I must get one."

"We'll see about that when we get back across the border. Question is, what do we do about those three?"

"We can ambush them," the Navajo suggested. "This road is deserted, apart from us."

"Yeah, but we don't have legal cause to shoot them – at least, not yet. I don't want to have to argue with the *Guardia Rural* about that. On a road like this, where we can see a long way, others can see just as far. We don't know whether anyone's watchin' us from off the road."

"True. Perhaps when we turn into the foothills, to follow that valley?"

"Perhaps, but again, I want to be a long way from witnesses if we have to take them." Walt thought for a moment. "Let's push the pace a little. We can be in Santa Rosa by five. Let's ride through the town, and then turn off the road on the far side. Since they're hangin' that far back, they won't be able to see what we're doin'. I reckon they'll think we're going to sleep there. They'll probably wait until dark before they come in after us. If we keep low and ride towards the mountains, through the thicker bush, we can circle back and find the trail to that canyon while they're sitting outside town, waiting. With luck, we'll shake them off, or at least make them waste time looking for our tracks."

"Let us do that, *amigo,"* Nastas agreed.

IT WAS NEARLY nine o'clock before Hector learned what they needed to know. He came hurrying up to Esteban. "They rode through without stopping. A *campesino* at a *cantina* said he saw them turn off the trail on the far side of town, heading towards the mountains."

Esteban cursed virulently. "That means they knew we were following them, and they wanted to shake us off. Damn the luck! I thought we were far enough back that they wouldn't notice, particularly since we're only three now."

"What are we going to do?" Felix asked.

"We'll have to wait until morning. The best tracker in the world can't read tracks at night. We'll follow them until we find them. Don't forget, Sandoval told us to get him. If we come back without his head, he'll blame us."

The other two nodded slowly. Their boss was not the kind of man to take failure lightly, or forgive those who let him down.

BY MID-MORNING, Walt and Nastas had entered the horseshoe valley the old man had described. The trail, wide enough for only one horse, ascended the right side of the valley at a steep incline. In a couple of places, they had to dismount and lead their horses past an outcrop of rock or a thick bush that did not allow enough room for riders.

As the road curved at the horseshoe bend, Walt saw a rock on the inside of the trail. A rough cross had been scratched onto the surface. Wind and weather had already partly obscured it. In a few more years, it would probably be unnoticeable. *"Este es todo,"* he called back to Nastas. "This is the place. It's just as the old man described it."

They stood for a moment at the grave, looking down at it silently. Walt took off his hat, and raised his eyes to the sky. "Lord, I ain't much of a prayin' man, but Major d'Assaily did his duty as he saw it, an' did it as well as he knew how. He had guts, loyalty, and faith in his cause. I reckon there's too few like that these days. I'd be obliged if you'll please remember him kindly."

Silently he added mentally, *And if you're so inclined, I'll be real grateful if you'll please help me find what he buried. It'll make all the difference in the world to me, an' also to Tyler Reese, 'cause it'll help me partner with him in his cattle ranch. We both served the same cause as the Major, an' lost just about everything for it. We've had to pull ourselves up by our bootstraps. It'd be real nice to recover some o' what we lost.*

Leading the horses to let them breathe, they moved on around the bend. As they were about to start climbing the other side of the canyon, Nastas pointed. "Look! You can see down the valley from here. Aren't those three riders, just starting up the trail?"

Walt took out his spyglass and peered through it. "You're right. It's those three from yesterday. I recognize their hosses. They musta tracked us from town, all the way around and back. They're determined bastards, aren't they?"

Nastas nodded. "Are we far enough from witnesses up here?"

Walt grinned. "I reckon so – and I think I know just how to discourage 'em. Have they seen us, d'you think?"

"If we can see them, they can see us, *amigo.*"

"You're right. With luck, it'll make 'em eager enough that they'll push hard to catch up with us. They won't pay much attention to anything else. That's just the way I want 'em. Come on, let's get moving. I want to find the right place to give them a surprise."

ESTEBAN POINTED. "It's them! Look, the bastards are almost around the bend in the trail already!"

Felix spat in disgust. "They must be three miles ahead of us, and we can't make more than walking pace up this pass. We won't catch up today."

"We'd better, or the boss will have our hides! Come on. At least we know where they are now. When we get to the top, we can push our horses harder."

The three men spurred their horses up the trail, cursing as it grew steeper.

WALT PLACED A LAST SMALL ROCK, then stood back, surveying his work critically. "I reckon that oughta do it."

Nastas sniggered. "I'm glad you are my friend. You make a very bad enemy!"

"All right, let's head up the trail and around the rock there."

Nastas led all the horses up the path. Walt waited until they were clear, then began to uncoil what looked like a roll of thick string, laying it out in the ditch that ran along the inside edge of the trail. The black line was almost invisible unless one looked hard for it. He tucked it under grass and behind shrubs and bushes as he slowly made his way up the path and around a big rock that jutted out from the valley wall, about seventy feet above where he'd been working.

THE THREE MEN rounded the horseshoe bend, and paused for a moment to let their horses catch their breath.

"Can you see them?" Esteban called to Hector, at the head of the group.

Hector peered up the trail. "No, but the path twists and turns around outcroppings. They're probably near the top, or already over it."

"Then we've got to keep moving. There are other trails leading off this one, a few miles beyond that. We need to see if they take one. We daren't lose them again!"

WALT HALF-SAT, half-leaned against the canyon wall while Nastas peered over the big rock sheltering them from sight. "They are turning onto the straight stretch. They'll be at the rocks in about a minute."

"All right." Walt reached into his pocket and took out a match. He held it ready, waiting.

Nastas asked, "What made you bring dynamite with you?"

"I used it to help kill some of the men who'd kidnapped your daughter, remember? It was real useful in taking their boss, too. Since then, I've always carried a few sticks on long journeys. A man never knows when it might come in handy."

The Navajo laughed softly. "I doubt those three will think of it as 'handy', *amigo.*"

"I doubt they'll be thinking of anything!"

"They are almost there... another ten feet... now! *Now!*"

Walt struck the match against his boot, and held its sputtering, hissing flame to the end of the fuse wound around his hook. Bickford's quick match was guaranteed to burn at a measured rate of thirty yards per second in still air. The spark flashed down its length, vanishing around the rock so fast the eye could barely follow it.

The four sticks of dynamite Walt had buried blew up with a thunderous blast that echoed from side to side, up and down the valley. A billow of black smoke and dust erupted from the valley wall. The stones Walt had piled over the dynamite turned into makeshift grapeshot, slashing out in all directions. Felix, in the center of the group, took the full force of the explosion. His body and his equally dead horse went flying off the path into the valley. Hector, ahead of him, was also killed by the stones. His grievously injured mount plunged off the path, rolling kicking and screaming down the steep side of the canyon, taking his body with it, breaking its neck in its fall.

Esteban, at the rear of the group, came off lightest. He was hit by a couple of flying stones, bruising him and drawing blood. His horse reared up in fright, tossing him from the saddle and pulling its reins out of his hand. It turned, kicking, bucking and pitching, and plunged back the way it had come, neighing and screaming its pain and fear.

Esteban landed hard, knocking the breath out of his body. The blast had deafened him, and shaken him to the core. It took him precious seconds, gasping for air, to realize that his only means of escape was running away as fast as it could move. "*¡Oye!*" he bellowed, in his shock ignoring everything else – including the possibility that whoever had set off the blast was still nearby. "Come back here!" He set off after the horse at a shambling run.

Above the rock further up the path, Nastas drew a bead on the stumbling figure through the sights of his new Winchester 1873 rifle. His finger caressed the trigger, and the shot went off with an abrupt bark and a billow of white smoke from the muzzle. The flat-nosed two-hundred-grain .44 bullet, propelled by forty grains of powder, slammed into Esteban's upper spine, severing it. The *bandido* pitched forward onto his face, dead before he hit the ground.

"Got him!" Nastas called down in profound satisfaction. "Thank you for another chance to ride the war trail, brother! That is the first blood for this new rifle. You got the other two with the dynamite. They won't be bothering us any more."

"What about that horse?" Walt asked.

"It will make its own way out of the pass in due course. The first *campesino* to find it will strip off the saddle and bridle and sell them, keep the rifle for hunting, and use the horse to pull his plow or his cart. The buzzards, coyotes and other carrion-eaters will soon take care of the others, hiding the evidence. I'll tip the last one's body off the path, to join his friends. The next few rains will turn the hole where the dynamite went off into mud, and slowly fill it. I don't think anyone that matters will ever figure out what happened."

"Let's hope so. I reckon they'll see the smoke and dust of the explosion in Santa Rosa, but they probably won't realize what it was, and the noise won't carry that far. All right, *amigo*. Tip that body into the canyon, then let's make tracks."

W ALT USED the diary's description to follow the path along the spine of the foothills. He counted off two trails that led down side valleys, then moved more slowly, scanning the countryside carefully as the sun dropped towards the western horizon. He used Major d'Assaily's compass to take bearings at intervals. At last he halted his horse.

"I can see Rancherias over there, almost due east," he said, pointing. "As for Santa Rosa, it's about north-north-east of here.

That means the valley where the Major buried his message must be this one here. He said he used the top of the southern wall – that one right there. The trail goes along that ridge, then seems to turn down into a valley over that way."

"Are you going to look for it tonight?"

"No. The light's fading fast. Let's make camp, get a good meal and a night's sleep, then start fresh in the morning. We'll have to move carefully down the trail, looking for a triangular shaped rock about halfway down the ridge. If we find one, I reckon that'll be the place."

They found a sheltered spot some distance from the trail, with rocks to hide the light from their fire. Nastas built it while Walt picketed the horses and off-saddled them. They shared a quick supper of bacon, beans and johnnycake, washed down with black coffee. They took it in turns to stay awake during the night, guarding against unexpected and unwanted visitors.

It rained lightly during the small hours of the morning. By dawn they were tired, cold, and aching from the damp in the air. They brewed more coffee, ate a hurried breakfast of the remains of last night's meal, and saddled their horses; then they headed down the ridge, riding slowly and carefully. Nastas watched ahead and behind, in case more *bandidos* showed up, while Walt looked for the triangular rock.

He found it halfway down the ridge, almost exactly as the Major had described it. "There it is!" he exclaimed, pointing to the right side of the trail. It was set back about ten feet, with bushes growing on two sides of it. They'd probably taken root since the gold had been buried there, nine years before. He used the compass to confirm that the towns of Rancherias and Santa Rosa de Múzquiz were on the correct bearings.

"I guess this is the right rock, Nastas." He hesitated. "I'm not too worried about more people coming up our back trail, because we took care of them yesterday; but they may still come from the other direction. Would you keep your eyes peeled, while I dig, and keep your rifle handy? I can lift this rock on my own, even with one hand, and I reckon what's under it won't have been buried deep. The Major didn't have time for that, what with being chased and all, and being wounded too."

"I shall do so, *amigo*."

Walt got down from his horse, took a spade from his pack horse, and walked over to the rock. He saw with satisfaction that Nastas was scanning up and down the mountainside, looking for any potential threat. He jammed the end of the spade beneath one end of the rock, placed a small stone beneath the base of the handle to act as a fulcrum, and put all his weight on it. With a sucking sound, the rock lifted up from the place where it had lain, revealing black, fertile soil. Walt lifted it further with his hand and hook, and leaned it against the bushes.

He took the spade and began to dig carefully into the ground. On his third scoop of earth, he felt something harder beneath the spade, and scraped away the thin layer of dirt. The edge of a leather container of some sort became visible, and he used his hook to pull on a strap at its edge. Slowly, almost reluctantly, the earth let go of what proved to be a leather pannier from a pack saddle. Walt pulled it out of the hole. It chinked softly as he laid it on the ground. Further investigation revealed a second pannier, which he also extracted.

Inside each pannier were two drawstring canvas bags, treated with oil and wax to make them as weatherproof as possible. Trembling in anticipation, Walt tugged at the drawstring of the first bag, pulled it open, and couldn't restrain a whoop of glee. The gleam of gold coins, undimmed by years of burial, met his eyes. Exultant, he picked up a handful and let them trickle through his fingers.

He didn't open the other three bags. It was obvious what they contained. He took them out, then checked the panniers for anything else. One contained a flat package wrapped in oilskin, presumably the letter from President Davis to Brigadier General Shelby.

He looked up at Nastas. "We've found it! This is what we came for."

The Navajo grinned broadly. "That is good. We have not wasted this journey, then." He showed no curiosity about what Walt had dug up, content to continue his scan for enemies.

"You don't want to look?"

"I heard the sound of coins, but that is only money. You white men are more concerned with that than I am. Now, if it were prime horses, that would be real wealth!"

Grinning at his companion's comment, Walt loaded the four canvas bags of gold and the oilskin package onto his pack saddle, transferring some of its other contents to Nastas' pack horse to balance the load between them. He replaced the leather panniers in the hole, scraped the dirt back over them, and lowered the stone once more, trying to make it appear undisturbed. There was no sense in letting anyone suspect that something had been dug out from under it.

At last he swung into the saddle. "All right, let's make tracks. My map doesn't show this trail – it's too small – but it's heading in the right direction, out of the mountains, and we can see Rancherias from here. The road to Monclova is east of the town. Once we're out of the foothills, we'll find it easily enough."

Nastas booted his rifle. "Lead the way. I shall follow."

It was late afternoon by the time they emerged at the head of a long, gently sloping valley at the base of the mountains. The trail widened as it ran out towards the flatlands. Some distance ahead on the right, there was a large white adobe ranch building, with stables, barns and storehouses around it. A shoulder-high adobe wall surrounded it at some distance, with a large gate arch providing entry. Workers' cottages were off to one side. A series of corrals stood on the other side, with horses in many of them, and more horses grazed in pastures on the right side of the valley. Clearly, this was a horse ranching operation of some sort.

Nastas borrowed Walt's spyglass and looked carefully at the nearest horses. "These are very fine animals, much better than most we have seen. They remind me of the old Spanish stock that I seek to breed true back home."

"Oh? Let me take a look." Walt held out his hand for the spyglass, and peered through it. "You know, you're right! I haven't seen so much horseflesh that good in years. I wonder if they're selling any?"

"Shall we ride to that *estancia* and ask?"

"I don't see why not."

They continued down the trail until they saw a path leading off it towards the *estancia*. Turning onto it, they couldn't help noticing that a man in a watchtower next to the house rang a bell, which came faintly to their ears, and leaned out and yelled something. Within a matter of moments, four men came to the gate, walking fast or running. They carried rifles. They didn't stand in the path, but appeared to take position on either side of the gate.

"They are cautious, *amigo*," Nastas noted.

"In this part of the world, I would be, too. We've already met some of the reasons why."

As they drew nearer, Walt could see the men peering over the wall. Only one appeared to be young. The others had gray hair to at least some extent, and one was almost bald. Their faces were lined and weatherbeaten. They didn't aim their rifles, but stood with them ready in their hands.

One of the men stepped into the gateway as they drew up their horses. "*Quién eres y qué quieres?*" he asked bluntly, without preamble. "Who are you and what do you want?"

Walt's eyebrows rose in surprise at so unfriendly a greeting. He said slowly, "We are travelers. I am here in Mexico to buy horses. We could not help noticing yours, and their high quality. We came to ask whether any were for sale."

The other man's lips formed an 'O' of surprise. "How did you get here? They did not stop you?"

"Stop us? Who? I don't understand, *señor.*"

"There are armed men who stop horse buyers and dealers from coming here." He waved his hands towards the eastern exit to the valley.

"We did not come that way, *señor.* We came down from the mountains to the west."

His face cleared. "Aha! That explains it. I am sorry for my less than polite greeting, *señor.* We have troubles these days. We thought you were among those who torment us. If you come to the *casa,* Don Thomas will want to meet you. This is his *estancia.*"

Walt and Nastas walked their horses behind the man as he led them to a hitching rail in front of the house. Another man ran ahead of them to warn those inside that they had visitors. The remaining two guards, both older men, waved amiably at the sentry in the watchtower, then ambled back to the stables, carrying their rifles casually resting over one arm.

As they dismounted, Walt heard the front door of the house swing open. He looked up, and caught his breath in astonishment. A young woman stood there, long dark red hair framing an attractive, freckled, lightly sun-tanned face. Her eyes were a mesmerizing green. She appeared to be in her late teens or early twenties. She wore a white blouse, cut high to preserve modesty, and a long flowing green dress that appeared to use less fabric than was fashionable. As she stepped forward, Walt realized that it was a divided skirt, designed to allow her to ride a regular saddle rather than a side-saddle. He'd heard of them, but never seen one before.

"Saludos, señores," she began. "Welcome to the *estancia* of Don Thomas O'Halloran. I am his daughter, Colleen. I am told you wish to discuss buying horses. I shall take you to his study. I

handle the *estancia*'s business affairs, so I shall be part of your discussions."

Walt found his heart beating unaccountably faster. This woman... something about her... he realized with a start of astonishment that he had been staring into her eyes for several seconds without saying a word. He flushed. "My apologies, *señorita*. I had not expected to see such beauty in the hinterlands of Mexico. I am Walter Ames, a horse rancher from Colorado, and this is my companion, Nastas, a horse breeder of the Navajo nation."

Now it was her turn for a hint of color to rise to her cheeks. "Beauty is where you find it. Come with me, please. Your horses will be cared for, and your saddlebags and pack saddles will remain undisturbed."

Strangely, Walt felt no anxiety about the gold on his pack saddle. Something about this place and its people just felt right. He handed the reins of his horse to the man who'd led them to the house, and Nastas did likewise; then they followed the woman into the house.

She led them through an imposing hall, rising fifteen to twenty feet above their heads, with whitewashed walls, paved with dark red tile. Several doors led off it. She went up to one and knocked gently. "Father, we have visitors."

"Bring them in, Colleen."

"*Si, papa.*" She gestured to them. "In here, please."

Thomas O'Halloran proved to be white-haired, tall, with a sunken frame revealing the ravages of time, even though he didn't appear elderly. He struggled to his feet from behind his desk and came around it to greet them, walking slowly and unsteadily. He must once have been a strong, powerful man, Walt thought as his daughter introduced them, and they shook hands. His face was shockingly disfigured, a big letter 'D' branded into his right cheek. Walt recognized it at once. *When did you desert from the U.S.*

Army?, he thought to himself. *That's how they used to mark deserters.*

"You are Navajo?" O'Halloran asked Nastas, still speaking Spanish. "I've heard that some of you are trying to preserve the bloodline of the horses that came here from Spain."

"Yes, *señor*. I am one of them. My family and I have a small herd of about fifty head at my home in northern New Mexico. We've tried to breed for quality, rather than quantity. This man, *señor* Walt, does the same, and we are sharing our breeding stock with him. I recognize some of the traits of our horses in yours. Are they also of the Spanish line?"

"Yes, they are. I've tried to build up the the finest breeding herd of that bloodline in all Mexico."

"I think you have succeeded, *señor*. From what we saw as we rode up, they are truly beautiful animals."

"But animals with no future, unless a miracle happens," his daughter said sourly, anger twisting her mouth as they sat down.

"Sadly, Colleen is right," her father admitted. "That's why you were met by suspicious, armed men, rather than a warmer welcome. There's a man who's determined to get his hands on my horses, and sell them to racing stables in Mexico City. There, they'd be ridden to death within a year or two. They use them hard, racing them several times every week, then discard them when they wear out. Often they end up being shot out of hand, their wind broken and their spirits too. I'll be eternally damned if I allow that to happen to mine!"

"Yes," his daughter confirmed. "Sandoval hired a bunch of *bandidos,* who set up camp outside our canyon at the beginning of the year. They refuse to allow any horse buyers to get in, and won't let us out to buy supplies. They're trying to starve us into submission, forcing us to sell out, horses, *estancia* and all, for a pittance. We've been able to send men with packhorses through the mountains to get some supplies, but they can't bring in enough for all our needs."

Her father added. "It's also a burden for our people. Most of those who work here came with me from America after the 1846 war. That's where I got this," and he touched the brand on his cheek. "I fought with the San Patricio Battalion."

Walt instantly understood the unspoken implication. He said softly, "I fought the U.S. army as well, or at least the Union Army. I served in the Confederate States Army during the Civil War. I was a sergeant, a scout and courier."

O'Halloran's eyes brightened. "I was a sergeant too! There were a bunch of soldiers, Irish immigrants like myself, who couldn't stomach the way we were treated because we were Catholic. We deserted, and formed the San Patricio Battalion to fight for Mexico instead, because it was a Catholic nation. We lost, of course, as you did too. Many of us were taken prisoner. If we deserted before the war, we were branded. Those who deserted after war was declared were hung as traitors." He sighed. "There are few of us left now."

Colleen interjected gently, "Father, about the horses?"

"Yes, yes, of course. Before we discuss them, would you gentlemen like to take a closer look at them? Colleen will tell you everything you want to know. While she's doing that, I'll have two guest rooms prepared for you."

Nastas looked surprised. As an Indian, he was used to being fobbed off with second-rate, servant's accommodation. O'Halloran obviously understood his expression, because he added, "Any breeder of Spanish horses is welcome in my house, *senor* Nastas. I have no prejudice against Indians. My late wife, Samanta, was one-quarter Kickapoo."

"I see. Thank you, *senor*."

Colleen flushed. Walt understood at once why she reacted that way. The lightly tanned look to her skin that he'd noticed before, and found attractive compared to the fashionable pallor often encountered on women in the United States, was now revealed as genetic rather than sun-caused. She might be described as an octoroon in American terms, he realized. She probably worried that he would now treat her as a person of mixed race, generally looked down upon in polite society. He wondered how he could dispel that fear, but said nothing for now. He'd let his actions speak for his attitude.

She rose to her feet. "If you'll come with me, *señores,* I'll take you to the horses. Jaime and Valerio can tell you more about them. They help with maintaining the bloodlines and planning our breeding program."

10

A s they walked towards the stables, and a servant hurried ahead to alert the hands that they were on their way, Colleen said bitterly, "Even if you buy some of our horses, I don't know how you'll get them out of this valley. Those *bandidos* will just take them away from you."

Walt smiled. "We might have something to say about that, *señorita.*"

"Just two of you? Against six of them?"

Nastas laughed. "Only six? They should have brought more!"

Her eyes widened with new hope. "You're serious? You really think you can get past them?"

"With a little bit of luck, we'll do more than just get past them," Walt promised.

"What do you mean?"

"I'll say no more at present, *señorita.* Let's look at the horses first."

She led them into a barn, where two men came forward and were introduced as Jaime and Valerio. Walt shook their hands, but was distracted by something standing in front of two wagons at the rear of the building. He pointed. "Do my eyes deceive me, or is that a U.S. Army mountain howitzer? The 12-pounder 1841 model?"

Jaime laughed. "Yes, it is, *señor*. It is a small souvenir of Don Thomas' service, you understand."

"It's got a prairie carriage, too, so it can be towed, instead o' havin' to be taken apart to move on muleback. Does it work?"

"It works very well. We have used it to keep our unwanted *bandido* visitors at a distance. We do not have many men, you see, *señor,* so this helps strengthen our defenses. Don Thomas taught us how to use it. I am in charge of its crew when needed."

"Do you have all the rounds for it – cannonball, case shot, canister and grapeshot?"

"*Si, señor,* although not many are left. It is hard to find them in Mexico."

Colleen sniffed. "If you've both finished looking at the cannon, perhaps Jaime can tear himself away from it to talk about our horses?" The men laughed, but took her point.

Walt allowed Nastas to walk ahead of them, talking animatedly with the two Mexicans and running his hands over the superbly conformed horses. He said thoughtfully, "*Señorita,* if we manage to get rid of the *bandidos* out there, that would not be the end of your troubles, I think."

"No." Her lower lip trembled for a moment. "I... I don't know how we can have any future here. After the French invasion, and the Juarez uprising against them, the *bandidos* have grown into a plague in many provinces, including this one. If we get rid of that bunch, others will come. My father is very ill. He cannot live much longer. I would like to run this place, as I have for some years already, but..."

"But the men will not obey a woman alone? They want a man to lead them?"

"The men we have will follow me, but the younger ones we need to hire will not. They think a woman should be married, with a man to manage business matters." She grimaced. "It's so unfair! I've run this place on my own already for so long!"

Walt sighed. "Yes, it is unfair. My late wife and I were partners in my businesses, and we worked together as equals. Sadly, Mexicans seem to place more store on what they call *machismo* than I do."

"Your wife died?"

"It's a long story, but she was murdered almost two years ago."

She drew in her breath with a gasp. *"Murdered?* How terrible! What did you do then?"

"I went after the men responsible, and killed them all." Walt's voice was flat and hard, with an edge of savagery to it that he didn't realize he was projecting.

"And you've been alone since then?"

"Yes. I'd very much like to marry again, but I want a partner, someone to stand beside me and work with me, like Rose, my first wife. There aren't many women who aspire to that."

"What sort of work do you do, *señor?"*

"I own a transport and freight company, and a ranch that I'm setting up to breed quality horses. That's one of the reasons I'm here in Mexico, to buy breeding stock for it. I daresay I'll have more ventures in due course. I'm talking to a friend about investing in a big cattle ranch in what's now Comanche and Kiowa country, as soon as peace is established."

"So you're a wealthy man?"

"I don't know about wealthy, but I'm doing all right."

"I see." She thought for a moment. "You're traveling with a Navajo. You feel no prejudice against Indians?"

"Nope." He grinned. "I have an Indian name myself, given to me by Satank of the Kiowa. That's a long story, so I won't go into details now. Basically, I judge anyone, no matter what their skin color or language or culture, by what they are inside, and how they behave. A good person is a good person, no matter what else they are. Same goes for a bad person, I guess."

"I wish more people thought like you." Her voice was bitter.

Walt guessed that she was probably still unmarried because of prejudice against those of mixed blood. It was possibly worse in Mexico, among the landed gentry, than it was in the United States. They'd regard her as suitable to be the mistress of some important man, but never his wife. He opened his mouth to say something, then closed it again. It wasn't his place to ask questions about that. If she wanted him to know something, she'd tell him.

Nastas turned to him, eyes alight with excitement. "*Amigo,* I have never seen better horses than these!"

Walt winced slightly. By letting his enthusiasm show so clearly, Nastas had probably driven up the price. He said only, "They sure do look good. *Señorita,* shall we return to the house and talk business?"

"By all means."

Walt watched her as she walked ahead of them, her slim, trim body swaying gracefully. He realized he was already more than a little smitten by her. He tried to tell himself to slow down, to take things gently... but he knew already that it would be very hard to do so.

Don Thomas greeted them as they came back into his study, and ordered a servant to bring coffee. "What did you think of my horses?" he asked as they sat down.

Nastas shook his head. "I have never seen finer, *señor.*"

The old man flushed with pride. "It's taken almost thirty years, but yes, I do believe we've done the breed proud. How many were you interested in buying?"

Walt held up his hand. "Before we talk numbers, *señor,* your daughter mentioned that your future on this *estancia* is probably not very bright, due to the *bandidos* and the unrest that still plagues Mexico. Would you agree?"

Don Thomas frowned, but nodded. "Yes, I do. That's why we haven't bred our mares for over a year, because we couldn't be sure the foals would be able to grow up undisturbed, or that we'd find a market for them. I'm in poor health. When I'm gone, I don't know how Colleen will be able to run this place. She's unmarried. Many men in these parts won't obey a woman's orders. However, if she marries, her husband will expect to take over and run it the way he sees fit. It's very unlikely he'll know as much about horses and the original Spanish bloodlines as she does, so he may make the wrong decisions, and run it into the ground."

His daughter's eyes flashed fire. "That's assuming I'd marry someone like that in the first place! All they want is a little woman at home to keep up the house, entertain their guests, and provide children at regular intervals. I won't be a brood mare for anyone!"

"I don't blame you, *señorita,*" Walt assured her. He turned back to her father. "I suppose the future of your workers also worries you?"

"Very much. Most of them came here from the United States, where they were *mesteñeros* and *vaqueros* in what is now Texas. I hired them because they knew so much about horses, and told them to bring their families with them. At one time we had over fifty people living and working here. Now, with their children grown up and moved away, the older ones have nothing to look forward to. I worry greatly about them, but I don't know what to do for them."

Walt nodded slowly, mind racing. "What if I could offer a future for your horses, and your workers as well, *señor?* I might even be able to offer one to you and your daughter, too."

Don Thomas and Colleen jerked upright. "A future? What do you mean?" he asked.

"I told Colleen that I have a ranch in Colorado, where I plan to breed horses. I came here to buy breeding stock, among other things. If the price is right, I'll consider buying your entire herd. What's more, I'll hire all your people, and help them move to Colorado. If they can prove that they were born in what is now the United States, there'll be no problem. They can continue to look after your horses, and teach my ranch hands all that you've taught them. I'll build houses for them, and they can live there as long as they please, even in retirement. Furthermore, if you and your daughter would like to move with them, I'll give you a home either on the ranch, or in Pueblo, the nearest city, where I also live much of the time. You can decide for yourselves. Of course, you'll be relatively well off, because I'm sure you won't sell your horses cheaply; so that money will let you live anywhere you please."

There was a long silence. Don Thomas and his daughter gazed, first at him, then at each other. There was a dawning hope in her eyes, a silent longing. Her father nodded slowly. "If... if that can be made to work... it would open up a whole new future for all of us, but especially for Colleen. I'd almost lost hope of one for her until now. What sort of price were you thinking of paying for my horses?"

"What do you normally ask for them, *señor?* I don't want to gouge you."

"I usually get the equivalent of a hundred to a hundred fifty dollars per horse."

Walt was astonished. That was far less than he'd expect to pay for animals of such high quality in the United States. Two to three times higher would be more like it. He managed to say, "Those prices are acceptable to me, *señor.* How many horses have you?"

Colleen answered, eyes bright with new hope, "We have seventy mares of breeding age and five stallions, plus three dozen working horses. They'd be much cheaper, of course."

"Of course. Shall we average the prices you quoted, and say one hundred and twenty-five dollars per breeding horse, stallion or mare?"

Don Thomas coughed explosively. He struggled to catch his breath, and Colleen hurried to his side, pounding his back, her face concerned. At last he recovered himself. "Young man, you do realize you're talking about more than nine thousand dollars?"

"Yes, I do, *señor,* and I have that much available, in gold."

The old man and his daughter stared at him, speechless, as if he were some sort of heavenly apparition appearing before them. There was a long silence.

Walt noticed that Nastas was looking at him, an appealing expression on his face. He grinned. *"Amigo,* you said that horses were real wealth, rather than money. Do you think ten of those breeding mares out there, plus one of the stallions, would make you rich?"

"Yes! A thousand times yes! They'll improve the bloodline of my herd so much that I hardly know how to say it."

"Then you may take your pick of them, once we get them safely back across the border. You've more than earned them, by helping me get here."

Nastas nodded solemnly, unable to speak, but the gleam in his eyes said it all. He held out his hand, and Walt shook it firmly.

Don Thomas managed to say, "And my people? How will you get them, and the horses, safely over the border?"

"I think we'll manage that easily enough. Do you have someone who can ride fast and hard for Monclova? I need to get a message there as quickly as possible."

Colleen said, "There's Felipe. He's the youngest of our men, and a good rider. We can give him extra horses, to ride relay. It's about sixty miles from here, so he can do it in a day if he has to, provided the horses are given time to recover afterwards."

"Very good. We'll send him off first thing in the morning. I'll send a message to a friend of mine, who's holding my other men in Monclova waiting for me. I'll have him hire trustworthy men there, and send them here to protect you while you pack up your goods and prepare for the journey. I'll also have him buy wagons and teams, one for each family of your workers, and as many as you need for yourselves, and send them up."

Colleen shook her head. "The *bandidos* will shoot Felipe rather than let him pass."

"Oh, no, they won't. You're going to tell us where they are, then Nastas and I are going to pay them a little visit after sunset. He and I will stay on here for a few days until my friend's men get here, just in case more *bandidos* arrive."

Nastas laughed. "Oh, it is good to be with you, my friend! Two fights in two days! My warriors will be so envious when I tell them!"

COLLEEN and her father stood on the porch of the *estancia,* staring out into the gloom of evening, straining their eyes and ears for any sign of activity. She shivered, pulling her mantilla around her shoulders. "Do... do you think they can do it, Papa?"

"That young man's a fighter, and so is that Navajo friend of his. I could see it in the way they move. I reckon those *bandidos* aren't going to know what hit them."

"But he has only one hand. How...?"

"Yes, but he's still a fighting man. They say there are no dangerous weapons, only dangerous people. Well, two hands or one, he'll be a dangerous man to his foes. I've seen his kind before."

"Then... is he safe, do you think? To be around, I mean."

"Oh, yes, I think so. The only people who won't be safe around him are those who choose to make him their enemy."

"He told me about his wife being killed, and how he hunted down those responsible. There was something in his voice... it chilled me."

"Don't fear that side of him, my daughter. I have it too, or had it when I was younger and stronger. You weren't there to know me back then, but I think I see something of my younger self in that man. I like him."

"And he's *rich!* To be able – not to mention willing – to spend almost twelve thousand dollars on horses, wagons and mules, plus wages for fighting men...!"

"He may be the answer to our prayers, Colleen. I'll be certain to thank the Blessed Virgin tonight, for sending him our way."

He glanced at his daughter. *I think he has an eye for you, too, my girl,* he thought to himself. *If you return his interest, I'll not be displeased. I think, for the first time, you may have met a man strong enough to match you, and not be dominated by you. He may be just what you need.*

Suddenly gunfire broke out in the distance, a rapid tattoo of explosions. A few faint winks of muzzle-flash could be seen in the dusk.

"Is that them?" Colleen exclaimed, clutching her father's arm.

"I think so. I daresay our *bandidos* just met their match," he replied, smiling broadly. "Be quiet, now, and listen."

They waited. The gunfire died down, and there was silence for a moment; then three more shots rang out, spaced evenly.

"That's the signal! They've done it!" he enthused.

"But are they all right?" she asked, real concern in her voice.

"We'll find out when they get back."

They stood in silence, waiting, for almost fifteen minutes, until they heard the faint clip-clop of approaching hooves. Colleen said, voice trembling, "Is that them? They left on foot!"

"Yes, but the *bandidos* had horses. I daresay they borrowed a couple of them."

Sure enough, Walt and Nastas appeared at the gate, and rode inside. They held Winchester rifles in the crooks of their arms, and drove four horses ahead of their mounts. Walt waved cheerfully as they approached.

"It's over," he said as they swung down from their saddles. "There were six of them, as you said." He gestured to the gunbelts slung over the saddles of the four horses they'd driven, and the rifles in the six saddle boots. "We brought their guns back, in case your men need them, and their horses, too, since we'll need them as remounts. We'll go out with a wagon in the morning to collect their bedrolls and other gear, and bury the bodies."

Don Thomas asked, "How did it go?"

"They were gathered around their camp fire, staring into the flames. That destroyed their night vision. Nastas and I shot the first two before they knew we were there, and the second two while they were still grabbing for their guns. That left only two more, and they were night-blind, so they couldn't see clearly to shoot at us. They didn't last long."

Colleen laughed aloud with relief. "So Felipe can head out at dawn?"

"He sure can. I'll write that letter now."

WALT AND NASTAS stayed at the *estancia* for three more days. No more *bandidos* appeared to replace those they had shot, but that didn't surprise Don Thomas. "They usually switch them out at weekends," he explained. "Those had only just arrived."

"Well, by the time their replacements get here, they'll find a lot more waiting for them than they bargained for," Walt retorted with a grin.

He spent as much time as he could with Colleen during those days. She invited him to accompany her for rides around the *estancia,* to show him its boundaries and how they had divided the horses among its pastures. He accepted with alacrity, not noticing the grins on the faces of Don Thomas and Nastas. They were in no doubt about what was happening.

Each evening after supper, Walt escorted Colleen for a walk in the twilight. She took the opportunity to speak English while they were alone, rather than the Spanish that was the *lingua franca* around the *estancia.* They talked about their respective childhoods, growing up in Tennessee and Mexico; what they had done in their lives so far; and what they hoped to do. She explained that after her father had suffered a heart attack, five years before, she'd taken over the running of the ranch, and since then had served as its business manager.

"My wife did much the same for me, although not because of illness," Walt told her. "Rose was a schoolteacher before we married. She kept the books and looked after the paperwork in a gun store we owned in Kansas. When I started the transport business in Colorado, she helped Samson, my depot manager, learn his way around it, and helped keep the books as well. When I was out with a wagon train, or hunting up business, she managed things in my absence. She was my strong right arm, and I've missed her help more than words can say. I've hired a manager to do a lot of what I used to do before I started the ranch, and he's very good, but it's not the same as having a wife to help me. I knew Rose so well, I could tell what she would think or do without her having to tell me, and she could do the same with me. That sort of shared trust was worth gold to both of us."

"She sounds like a very special woman." Colleen's voice was wistful.

"I think she was. It... it hurts more than I can say to know that I may be partly to blame for getting her killed."

Colleen slammed to a halt, staring at him. "What do you mean?"

Walt explained about hanging four horse thieves who'd killed one of his men. "It had to be done. That's the way it is in the west; if you don't stand up for yourself, if you don't show strength, all the other bad men out there will be on you like wolves after a weak, sick deer."

She nodded. "It's that way here, too."

"Yes, but I also went after the man who'd sent those thieves. One of those I hanged was his son. I ended up burning down his house, to teach him a lesson. Trouble is, that pushed him over the edge. He wanted revenge so bad that, when he found out who'd done it, he came after me. Rose was killed when he attacked me. I've always blamed myself for that. If I hadn't hanged them, and gone after him, she might still be alive."

Colleen sighed. "Yes... but if you hadn't done that, you'd have made yourself a target for many more thieves. I don't see what else you could have done."

"Neither do I, but it still tears at me sometimes. I guess I'll just have to try to do better, and think more clearly, if I get another chance at happiness."

"I think the right woman will understand," she assured him, her eyes glowing softly.

He longed to kiss her, but forced himself to hold back. It was too soon. *Take your time,* he commanded himself sternly. *Let this grow at its own pace. Don't rush her.*

Late in the afternoon of the third day, the watchman in the tower rang his bell. "There is a party of men approaching fast," he called down. "There must be at least ten of them, maybe more."

Walt ran up the ladder, to take a look through his spyglass. "Relax," he called down. "It's Tyler Reese, and he's brought the men I asked for."

He hurried down, and was standing with Don Thomas, Colleen and Nastas on the porch by the time the new arrivals cantered through the gate and drew up in a long line before them. Tyler jumped down from his horse, doffed his hat to Don Thomas and Colleen with a flourish, and said to Walt, "I've brought the first of the men you asked for. More will come next week, with the wagons I ordered for you."

"Great!" Walt shook his hand enthusiastically. "Thanks for coming through for us." He introduced Tyler to Don Thomas and his daughter. "How did you find the men so quickly? They look good, a lot cleaner and better equipped than the *bandidos* we've seen so far."

"I remembered what you said about the *Guardia Rural*. They've got a regional headquarters in Monclova, so I went to see the *Comandante* and asked him to help me find good, reliable, trustworthy fighting men to deal with a *bandido* problem on an *estancia* up here. He was happy to help, and offered me one of his sergeants to represent the *Guardia*. I agreed, o' course, and promised the sergeant that we'd pay him in gold for his help. I bought some extra horses, too, so we could ride relay. We covered the sixty miles from Monclova in sixteen hours, starting before dawn today."

"You couldn't have done better. I'll repay you everything you spent. What about the wagons?"

"I've brought eleven men with me; nine local hired gun hands, my *segundo,* Tom Dixon, and the *Guardia* sergeant. Tom will be in charge of the men while you and I are gone. I've hired another eight men, and ordered a dozen six-mule wagons for you, as you asked, with their teams. They'll come from Monterrey. As soon as they reach Monclova, the eight men will escort them here, to make sure they arrive safely. Tom will pay them, then they can escort the wagons' delivery drivers back to Monclova. He'll stay on with his ten men until we arrive with the horses, to take everyone with us."

"You've gone to a great deal of trouble for us, *señor,*" Colleen said with a smile. "We are grateful."

"Indeed we are," Don Thomas agreed. "I'll have to send one or two wagons to nearby towns to buy supplies to feed you all, but with so many men on hand, I'm sure an escort won't be hard to arrange."

"No, it won't, sir," Tyler assured him. "They'll probably be hoping the *bandidos* try to interfere, so they can earn their pay!"

That evening, they made plans. Don Thomas agreed that everyone and everything would be packed and ready to go by the fifteenth of March. Walt would bring the last part of the horse herd to the ranch, stopping for a day or two to allow the horses to rest and eat their fill while last-minute packing and organizing took place; then everyone would travel to the border together.

From there, they would head for Fort Clark, then on to El Paso, and then to Colorado.

"It'll be a very long, tough journey," he warned them. "We'll move pretty slowly, to spare the horses. At twenty miles a day, that means we'll be on the trail for at least two months. Will everyone be able to stand the pace?"

"We'll have to, won't we?" Don Thomas growled. "It won't be the first long journey any of us have made. I long ago converted one of our celerity wagons into a bedwagon for my wife and myself, and later for our daughter too. We'll be comfortable in that. I'll get it overhauled and the wheel hubs greased."

"I reckon so," Walt agreed. "Rose and I converted a Rucker ambulance in the same way. We'll take oats with us, too, to feed to the working horses and mules, to keep their strength up. They're going to need it."

After supper, Walt followed Don Thomas and Colleen to the office. Together they counted out, from the gold Walt had recovered on the mountain, four hundred and sixty-nine twenty-dollar double eagle coins, the purchase price of Don Thomas' entire breeding herd. Walt added another three hundred dollars, fifteen coins, for the working horses.

Colleen stared at the piles of gold coins on the desk, twenty to a stack. "That's more money than I've ever seen in my entire life! Papa, does that mean we're rich?"

"We were always horse-rich and cash-poor, daughter. Now it's the other way around, thanks to this man. This will secure our future, and yours after I'm gone." He looked at Walt. "I'll never be able to thank you enough for this. You've given us all a new beginning."

"It's all still to do," Walt warned. "Let's get you over the border into America first, and then all the way up to Colorado."

"As you say, but I think we've made a very good start. We'll make sure to be ready for you when you return."

Walt was struck by a sudden thought. "You'll be bringing that cannon with you, won't you?"

"Yes, we'll break it down and load it on a wagon. Why do you ask?"

"If you were going to leave it, I'd have bought it from you. The idea of a personal cannon appeals to me."

Don Thomas grinned. "Perhaps I'll give it to you as a gift, for a suitable occasion." It wasn't hard to guess what occasion he was implying. He'd openly approved of Colleen and Walt spending time together.

Colleen went for a last walk with Walt that night, after everyone else had finished talking and was preparing for bed. They paced slowly in silence beneath the moonlight. At last she sighed. "I'm going to miss this place," she said slowly. "I mean... I'm very grateful to you for helping us out of our present trouble, and I'm looking forward to a new and much brighter future, but... my mother is buried in the churchyard at Rancherias. Papa says we should leave her there, in a place she knew and loved, with our friends around her, but... it feels like abandoning her. Besides, Papa bought a double grave plot. He always intended to be buried alongside her. If he goes to America, he probably won't be."

Walt sighed. "I understand. It's hard to break ties like that; but, if you stayed, you might have no future. I think your mother would prefer you to have a better one."

"Oh, of course! She'd be the first to tell me to seize opportunity when it came knocking. That's what she did when she married Papa. She left everything and everyone for him, and never looked back. They were very happy together." She smiled. "Speaking of missing things, I've already grown accustomed to walking with you like this in the evenings. I'm going to miss it... and you."

Walt said softly, "I'm going to miss you, too, very much."

She turned her head to look up at him. Very gently, he bent

and kissed her lips. She pressed hers against his, closed her eyes, and leaned into him for an endless moment as his hand pulled her gently to him and hugged her shoulders. Her arm stole around his waist, and tightened.

As he straightened up, she opened her eyes and said mischievously, "We've only done that once, but already I know I'm going to miss it as much as I'll miss you!"

He laughed. "When I come back, dare I hope for another?"

"You'll just have to hurry back and see, won't you?"

"You can count on that."

11

T he men Tyler had left in Monclova greeted their return with enthusiasm, and exclaimed in frustration at having missed two fights with *bandidos*. "Dang, boss, you're hoggin' all the fun to yourself!" one of Walt's ranch hands complained, to a chorus of agreement. "How about savin' some of 'em for us next time?"

"I daresay they won't be the last we'll run into down here," Walt reassured him.

They rested for another day to let Walt, Nastas and Tyler get over the sixty-mile journey from the *estancia*, which they'd covered in just one day, riding relay. Walt took the opportunity to visit the regional headquarters of the *Guardia Rural*, where he handed in the statements from the *alcalde* and citizens of Nueva Rosita and described what had happened there. He didn't bother mentioning his second encounter with the *bandidos* in the horse-shoe valley.

"You acted correctly, *señor*," the *Comandante* assured him after reading them. "Thank you for exercising restraint, and not shoot-ing. In such a crowd, that would have been very dangerous. Your bullets might have passed through the *bandidos* and hit innocent people. I understand you had more problems with *bandidos* at the *estancia* of Don Thomas O'Halloran? Your compatriot, *Señor* Reese, mentioned that when asking for my assistance."

"Briefly." Walt described what had happened, and handed over a letter from Don Thomas confirming the details.

The *Comandante* read it quickly, and nodded. "I see no reason to burden the *Guardia* with a pointless investigation. Thank you for assisting Don Thomas, *señor*. He is a good man."

"Yes, he is. Do you think the *bandidos* will try to hit him again?"

"They will be very foolish if they do. I helped *Señor* Reese choose the men he took there. They know how to use their guns, and are not afraid to do so."

"I'm glad to hear it."

That evening, Walt and Tyler sat down together to discuss the next few weeks. "It's gonna be a real frenzy," Walt warned. "We'll have to split up. Pablo's people organized a horse fair at the arena in Saltillo, and they reckon hundreds of sellers will be there. There's another fair in Monterrey, just outside the town, and there should be even more coming to that one. Will you take Monterrey, and I'll take Saltillo?"

"Sure. What about money?"

Walt grinned. "I found what Major d'Assaily had buried." He didn't mention the total amount. "I'll give you seven thousand dollars to buy horses, and you've got your three thousand. I'll add another two thousand for travel costs, to hire more men, and as a reserve. If the buyers want payment all in gold, with no greenbacks, then they've got to accept a lower price. I reckon you may be able to buy as many as a thousand all told, perhaps a few more. Vicente's *mesteñeros* are good judges of horseflesh, and you've got the Army's list of what it wants, so choose those you buy very carefully."

"Count on it. What about taking them north?"

"I was watching the grazing as we came south. It's not real

good out in the flatlands, although it's better nearer the mountains. We'd better not drive too many horses over the same route.
There won't be enough for them to eat. I think you'd better split
your herd in two, sending off four or five hundred head as soon as
you've bought and branded 'em, then following with the rest
when you're done. Head for Laredo, cross the border there, and
then go up to the east of the Rio Grande. The grass should be
better on that side of the river. Send your Navajo scouts out ahead
of the herds, to pick good grazing for each day's journey and the
next night's stop. For my part, I'll also split my horses into two
smaller herds, and send them to Piedras Negras via Monclova. I'll
take the second herd past Don Thomas' *estancia* to collect him
and his hands. We'll meet up at Fort Clark, to tally up the
numbers and sort out the money."

"Sounds more'n fair to me." Tyler's eyes twinkled. "Are you
gettin' sweet on that pretty girl at the *estancia?*"

"I guess I am. Does it show?"

"Only a lil bit, what with you trippin' over your own feet and
droolin' whenever she appears!" Walt mock-swung a fist at him,
and Tyler ducked, grinning. "Hey, you asked!"

"I guess I did. Yeah, I'm gettin' awful fond o' that young lady.
I've got hopes."

"I'll be rootin' for you, buddy. She looks to be worth it."

"What about you? You ain't married yet."

"Naw. I ain't found someone fool enough to put up with me
yet!"

As he settled into his bedroll that night, Walt did some quick
mental arithmetic. He'd recovered thirty-five thousand dollars in
gold from where Major d'Assaily had buried it, to add to the ten
thousand dollars he'd brought across the border. He'd spent
almost ten thousand of it to buy the horse herd from Don
Thomas' *estancia,* and committed another two thousand to buy
wagons and mule teams. That was an investment, of course; he'd
transfer them to Ames Transport in Pueblo when they got there.

He expected to spend a thousand or more on hiring hands over the rest of their time in Mexico, including the gunmen now guarding the *estancia,* those escorting the wagons, and the men he'd hire to get the horse herds from here to Fort Clark. Call it thirteen thousand dollars all told, plus another nine thousand to Tyler to buy horses and for expenses – twenty-two thousand in total.

That left him with twenty-three thousand dollars in hand. Even if he spent half of it to buy horses, he'd have done very, very well out of this trip – and there were still all the Army payments to come.

He mentally raised his hat to God. *I asked you to help me find what the Major buried, and you sure came through for me. I'm thankin' you. Now, if you don't mind me askin' another favor, would you please put the right thoughts in Colleen O'Halloran's head? I've grown awful fond o' her. It'd be nice to bring a wife back from Mexico, as well as horses. Who knows? She might even teach me to talk to you more often.*

He fell asleep with a smile on his face, dreaming of her lips on his.

THE ARENA at Saltillo was large, with rows of seats on all four sides. It was normally used for bullfights and other entertainments. Pablo's men had arranged to hire the entire place for two weeks, arena, stables, barns and all.

Walt was grateful for their forethought. "It's perfect!" he enthused to his men. "We can set up a circuit in here. As each hoss is brought in, it can be looked over by those who know what we want. If they turn it down, it can be taken out right away. If it passes, it comes to me, to look it over and offer a price. If the seller has more than one horse, we'll collect them in a group, and deal with him after they've all come through. When we've bought 'em, they'll be taken out back to where some of you will have brandin' irons hot. There's even a branding chute at the side of that corral, so we don't have to build our own. I reckon we can deal with several hundred horses each day, if we do this right."

He sent out the two members of Pablo's advance party who'd accompanied him, to look for more local hands; *vaqueros,* grooms, whoever had experience with horses and could prove themselves trustworthy in handling them gently and carefully. It took two days of interviews and practical tests to hire two dozen men. "I'll pay you twenty dollars in gold every month," he offered, "with a bonus of another twenty when we get to Fort Clark. You can expect to work for up to two months. That'll get you up to sixty gold dollars." They all accepted with alacrity, eyes gleaming at the prospect of wages double what they could expect to earn locally.

"We may have some trouble with *bandidos* or Indians as we drive the horses north," he warned them. "Bring your guns, and be ready to use them if you have to. That's part of your job." They didn't turn a hair at the prospect.

Walt appointed Vicente, who'd accompanied him all the way from El Paso, as his *segundo,* or second-in-command. "You'll help me here during the hoss buyin', then take the first half of the herd north," he told him. "I trust you to get them to Fort Clark in good condition. Remember, don't push them too hard, or they won't be at their peak when they get there. When you arrive, have the Army sign acceptance papers for them, and ask Colonel Mackenzie to hold the payment draft for me. I'll collect it when I bring the rest of the horses."

"*Si, señor.* It shall be done as you wish."

The first day began with a mad crush of horses and their owners, all of whom wanted to be first in line. Walt was forced to go outside several times, and bellow at them through a cone-shaped speaking trumpet. "We're here for a week, and longer if need be," he told them at the top of his lungs. "You don't have to worry. We won't run out of money. Take your time and wait your turn!" It didn't help much.

Ranchers, farmers and owners had brought their horses from a wide area around Saltillo; from Torreón, a hundred and fifty miles to the west, to San Tiburcio, a hundred and ten miles to the south, to Entronque San Roberto, eighty miles to the south-south-east, to Monclova, a hundred and twenty miles to the north. In that vast area, more than thirty thousand square miles in extent, tens of thousands of horses were to be found, and many of their owners urgently desired good Yankee dollars in exchange for them. That meant the crush of sellers was inevitable, Walt supposed, sighing to himself.

It soon became apparent that many of the sellers had not listened to the description of what Walt was looking for in a horse. More than half of those offered had one or more defects that would prevent their being accepted by the U.S. Army. Walt turned them away, refusing to be swayed by anguished pleas from their owners. He and the others rapidly became expert in how desperate owners could disguise defects or problems in their animals, from using dye or boot polish to conceal scrapes and scars, to putting thicker horseshoes, or regular horseshoes with wooden backing, on their hooves to make them look taller. Some sellers even tried to bring back the same animals on successive days, in the hope that they might find a different person inspecting them, and be able to fool him. It didn't work.

Walt also found that some shady characters took to hanging around outside the barn that he'd reserved for himself and his men. They were sleeping in the hayloft, while their saddles and pack saddles were stored below. He took the precaution of leaving at least three men on guard in and around the barn at all times, heavily and very visibly armed. He also visited the local *Comandante* of the *Guardia Rural,* handed him a letter of introduction he'd got from the *Comandante* in Monclova, and explained what he was doing in Saltillo. As a result, the *Comandante* obligingly –

for a small fee, payable in advance in gold – kept a detachment of his men on patrol at the fairgrounds, day and night. They proved a useful deterrent. Coupled with Walt's own armed guards, they kept the shady characters from trying too hard to get into the barn, or steal horses.

Despite all the problems, the horse buying process went forward. Walt found they could process up to a hundred acceptable horses a day, and turn away up to two hundred that didn't measure up to their requirements. Most sellers proved willing to accept a lower price in return for payment in gold, rather than paper currency. The branding crews worked late into the evening, cancelling existing brands on the horses and applying Walt's Rafter A brand instead. There were fewer really good horses than he'd expected. Only about one in thirty met his higher personal standards, and had its brand underlined to designate it as part of his future breeding stock. Even so, they weren't as good as Don Thomas' horses; but then, few of that quality were to be found anywhere.

By the end of five days, they had four hundred and seventy horses penned in the arena's corrals, eating a fortune every day in oats and hay. Walt said to Vicente that evening, "I think it's time you headed out. You've bought all the supplies you'll need?"

"*Si, señor,* and loaded them onto pack saddles. We'll put them on different horses every day, and switch riding horses the same way, to keep them all fresh and strong."

"All right. Tomorrow morning at dawn, you ride. You'll have fifteen men in all, which should be more than enough to handle the herd and deal with any *bandidos* or Indians who want to take them."

He and the others got up early to watch the departure. It was a thrilling spectacle for the locals, who had never before seen so many horses gathered in one place. More than five hundred animals set off from the arena towards the trail to Monclova. The dust from their hooves filled the air, and their neighing and snorting was deafening at close range.

As the last of the horses disappeared down the street, Walt turned to the rest of the men. "That'll be us, in a week or so's time. All right, let's get ready for another day's work."

He was interrupted at mid-afternoon the following day by a messenger from Tyler in Monterrey. He'd dispatched the first part of his horse herd, more than five hundred animals, to Laredo. He also reported that the mule wagons had arrived safely at Don Thomas' *estancia*. The drivers who'd delivered them had returned safely to Monterrey. "It's all looking good up there," he reported. "The *bandidos* tried to bring in more men to take the place of those you dealt with, but Tom and his boys gave them a warm welcome, then sent the survivors on their way. They haven't been seen or heard of since."

Walt couldn't help but smile. From what he'd seen of Tyler's *segundo* and the men he'd brought, he was confident that those *bandidos* had not been handled gently.

Another messenger the following day brought word from Don Thomas. He confirmed that the entire *estancia* and all its people would be packed and ready from the evening of March 15 onwards. "We aren't loading most of our furniture and the like," he advised. "Much of it is old, and it isn't worth taking. Thanks to your generosity in buying all our horses, I've been able to give each family a hundred dollars in gold. They'll use that to buy whatever they need when they build their new homes." Walt nodded. The gesture was what he'd expect from a respected patriarch like Don Thomas. He would look after his people, no matter what.

Don Thomas enclosed a note from Colleen. It had been dabbed with perfume, which Walt sniffed delightedly before opening it. Its scent did not escape the notice of those on either side of him. One mock-sneezed loudly. "Dang, boss, what *is* that?

You taken to wearin' ladies' smelly stuff now?" There was a roar of laughter from the others nearby.

"No, my feet always smell that good," Walt retorted, to more laughter and shouts of pretended outrage. "You're just jealous."

Nastas smiled. "If you had seen the lady *Señor* Walt met at the *estancia,* you would not wonder," he told them in Spanish. "Instead, you would long for her to write to you too."

"Beautiful, is she?"

"Like the sun rising out of the mist over the fields on a spring morning."

"Dang, that Injun's turned into a poet," one ranch hand muttered. "Must be somethin' in the water down here."

Nastas heard him. "No," he corrected, "it is the horses on that *estancia*. If you think we are buying good horses here, just wait until you see them. They are magnificent – enough to turn any horse breeder into a poet!"

Walt ignored them as he settled down to read. Colleen started almost formally, hoping that he was well, and that the horse buying was producing the quality of animals he was looking for. Then she turned coquettish. "I've packed most of my clothes. I've also packed the small trousseau my mother helped put together for me before she died, four years ago. Who knows? It may come in handy."

Walt grinned to himself. The little minx was teasing him, was she? Well, two could play at that game!

"I look forward very much to seeing you soon," she closed. "The memory of our last walk together is still fresh and enticing. I want to take another with you, as soon as we can."

He couldn't help a powerful physical reaction to her words. *Oh, lady, you have no idea what you're doing to me,* he thought – *or maybe you do. With luck, it won't be long before we can find out more about that side of each other.*

He settled down to sleep, tingling with anticipation at the thought.

THE NEXT FIVE days were a whirlwind of activity. Most of the sellers with sub-standard horses had by now accepted that they had no chance, so they took their animals home with them. However, that meant the remaining horses could not be rejected quickly, because they almost all deserved closer scrutiny. That slowed down the daily average. Walt found the most he could handle was up to a hundred and fifty horses per day.

The hands worked from sunup to sundown, feeding the growing herd in the corrals, watering them, and branding the new arrivals. There was no grass for the horses to graze, and there were not enough men to take them out of town to do so. They had to be fed hay and oats from local feed merchants, who were glad of the business, but soon began to run low. They had to send to ranches and farms all over the area to bring in fresh supplies, which caused feed prices to rise sharply. Walt could afford them, but some others found that difficult, and they complained about it.

Other businesses in town didn't care. They were making a lot of money catering to the needs of Walt and his men, and the many horse sellers who suddenly had money to spend. The horse fair caused a short-lived miniature economic boom in Saltillo, and everyone who could took advantage of it.

By three o'clock in the afternoon of the fifth day, it was over. The last horse was branded and put into a corral to join the rest of the herd. The hands gathered at the barn, sweaty, covered in dust and dirt, tired, but triumphant.

"We've bought another five hundred and seventy-seven horses," Walt told them. "We'll take tomorrow off, to let you catch up on your sleep, wash your clothes and yourselves, enjoy a drink in the saloons, and prepare for the drive north. Make sure you don't get drunk or cause any fuss, you hear me? If you get tossed in the hoosegow because you stepped over the line, I'm gonna leave you there!" Laughing and jeering at one another, the men promised to behave.

They trooped down to the nearest bathhouse, which had done a roaring trade every evening of the horse fair, and washed away the dust and dirt. Putting on clean clothing, most of the men headed for the saloons to celebrate. Walt went back to the barn, where he sat down with Angel, one of Vicente Romero's *mesteñeros,* to plan the journey north. They made a long list of supplies they'd need for the trip.

"All right," Walt said at last, stretching wearily. "I'll give you money in the morning. Buy all this, and have the men load it onto pack saddles. Use some of our herd as pack horses – they're all supposed to be broken to the saddle – and change them out each day, so we don't overtire them."

"I will, *señor.* Should we do the same with our riding horses?"

"Yes. Let's keep them all as fresh as we can, which means they only get used once, then swapped for another mount the following morning. Don't let the men pick favorite horses and keep riding them."

"No, *señor.*" Angel sipped his mug of black coffee. "Have we done as well as you expected, do you think?"

"I'd say we've done a lot better. I hadn't expected to find so many horses that meet what the Army wants, or to be able to afford them. I just hope Colonel Mackenzie comes through with the money for them!"

"I, too, *señor.*"

"All right, Angel. Go get some rest, and I'll do the same."

Two days later, in the half-light of dawn, Walt gathered the men together and reminded them of what to watch for on their journey. "In particular, take it easy with the horses," he warned them. "If they arrive at Fort Clark in anything but good condition, the Army won't buy them, and you won't get your bonuses. That's why we're limiting ourselves to twenty miles a day. It's slow, sure, but it spares the horses.

"We're heading to an *estancia* near Rancherias, about ten days' ride from here. We'll spend a couple of days there, to let the horses rest and graze – there's a lot of grass in that valley. After that, we'll be joined by a dozen wagons and more people, and we'll all go on to Piedras Negras and Fort Clark together. That'll take about seven days more. When the Army's paid me, I'll pay off all you local hands, and you can come home."

He waited until they were all in their saddles, then signaled to Angel to open the corral gates. "All right, move 'em out! Head 'em north!"

12

On the morning of the tenth day, Walt left Angel in charge, took Nastas with him, and rode out ahead of the herd towards the *estancia*. He was burning with eagerness to see Colleen again, and pushed his horse fast. Laughing, Nastas protested, *"Amigo,* you told us to be gentle with our mounts, yet here you are, driving yours as if *bandidos* were after you!"

Walt flushed. "You're right. I'm sorry." He reined in his horse to a more sedate trot.

"De nada. I understand why you are hurrying. I was that way, too, when I was courting my wife. Time not spent with her seemed like time wasted."

"That's about the size of it."

They came in sight of the estancia by early afternoon. From a distance, Walt could see that each of the worker's cottages had a wagon parked in front of it, clearly to carry that family's possessions. The mules were grazing in a group to one side of the house, watched over by two horsemen. However, the guards were not in evidence, apart from one manning the watchtower, who waved when he saw them. The place had an almost listless, uneasy air about it.

Nastas picked up on it as well. "I think something is wrong, *amigo,*" he warned.

"I dunno, but it's awful quiet compared to when we were here last. Let's find out."

They cantered through the gate and over to the main house. The sentry in the watchtower called down as they drew up, in a quiet voice, "Please don't make too much noise, *señores.* Don Thomas is very sick."

Walt signaled his understanding as they dismounted and tied their horses to the hitching rail. They mounted the porch and knocked at the main door. After a few seconds, it was opened by a maid, who blinked in surprise to see them.

"*Señor* Walt! You are back!"

"Yes. What's this about Don Thomas?"

The woman shook her head sadly. "He would not listen when his daughter told him not to work, but let others do the packing. Three days ago he fell down, clutching his chest. She put him to bed, and we sent for the doctor, but he said there is nothing he can do. Don Thomas has suffered another heart attack. The priest arrived this morning. He is with him now, and the *Señorita* Colleen also."

Walt's heart sank. "I... I'm very sorry. Would you please tell the *señorita* that I am here?"

"Yes, *señor.* If you would please wait in the hall?"

"I will."

As she turned away, Nastas said, "I'll wait outside. She will want to speak with you alone."

Walt looked at him gratefully. "Thanks."

A few moments later, Colleen came out of a door at the rear of the hall. "Walt!" She hurried over, almost running, and fell into his arms, clinging to him tightly. There were tears in her eyes. "Oh, thanks be to God that you're here! I was so *lonely,* trying to handle this without you!"

He held her tightly, bowing his head to kiss the top of hers.

"I'm real sorry I wasn't here to help you stop him trying to help. He should have known better."

"He did know better – he just didn't want to listen!" Her voice was sharp, almost angry, then she shook her head. "It's no use complaining. That's Papa, through and through. He never took a back seat to anyone before, and he wasn't about to start now."

"Can I see him?"

"He wants to see you. When Margarita came to tell me you'd arrived, he signed to me to bring you in. He can't talk much, but he's aware of us."

"All right. Let's go."

Colleen led him into what proved to be Don Thomas' bedroom. He was in a large four-poster bed, covered with a sheet, lying propped up against several pillows. A priest in a brown robe was seated next to the bed, fingering a rosary. He stopped and looked up as they came in.

"Papa, Walt is here. Padre Francisco, this is Walter Ames, from America. He's the man who bought our horses, and has offered us a new life in Colorado."

The priest inclined his head. He was an elderly man, thin and spare of build, his hair cut in a tonsure to indicate his clergy status. "Greetings, my son. Are you Catholic?"

"No, padre, but I'm Christian."

Walt crossed to the bed, picked up Don Thomas' hand, and squeezed it gently. He was horrified by its lack of strength and flaccidity. Clearly, Don Thomas was very weak.

He was struck by a sudden thought. He said, softly, gently, "Colleen, you know I have feelings for you. Am I right in thinking you share them towards me?"

She stiffened. "What – why are you asking me *now*, of all times, when Papa is so sick?"

"I'm asking *because* your father is so sick. It's for his sake as much as mine. Trust me. Well?"

She flushed. "Y-yes. Yes, I do return them."

"Thank you." He turned to Don Thomas. "I may never get this chance again, and a man should ask, if he can. Don Thomas, may I please have your daughter's hand in marriage?"

The old man blinked, and a slow smile spread over his face. He whispered, "Nothing would make me happier. Yes, you have my blessing."

Colleen burst into tears. "Oh, *papa!*" She leaned over the bed and hugged him.

Walt turned to the priest. "Padre, can you perform a wedding right here, right now, in this bedroom? It may be Don Thomas' only chance to give his daughter away."

The priest frowned. "According to the Church, marriage should be solemnized in a consecrated church or chapel, if one is available. My church is in Rancheria, so we cannot use the excuse that none is nearby."

Walt shook his head impatiently. "I'm willing to have another wedding in your church, if that's necessary: but Don Thomas is in no condition to get there. Would you consent to a provisional marriage here, to be confirmed at a second ceremony later?"

Padre Francisco thought for a moment. "It is most irregular, but I take your point. Very well. If you agree to a proper wedding ceremony in my church as soon as it can be arranged, I will do it. One thing, though, my son. If you are not Catholic, the Church requires that you give your consent for your children to be raised as Catholics."

"I don't say I won't encourage them to think for themselves once they grow up, padre, but I want them raised as Christians. I guess the Catholic Church can do that as well as any other."

Colleen had listened to their exchange. Walt looked down at her as she half-sat, half-lay next to her father. "Colleen, will you marry me here and now, so your father can be part of our wedding, and give you away?"

She smiled, a great beam of joy. "Oh, *Walt!* Yes! Please!"

"We will need at least two witnesses," the priest put in.

"No problem," Walt replied. "Let's get the heads of each of your workers' families in here. They can witness it, and tell the rest of your people about it, too."

Colleen jumped to her feet. "I'll have Margarita bring them here at once."

"I'm sorry," Walt said, embarrassed. "I'm wearing my dirty trail clothes, and I don't have anything better in my saddlebags."

"That's all right, darling." She used the endearment for the first time, and both of them blushed as they realized what she'd said. "God will understand. I'll put on a clean dress, though. I've been in this one all night and all today, looking after Papa."

"Sure, go ahead."

As she bustled out, Walt asked the priest, "What about marriage licenses and that sort of thing?"

"We can sort all that out before your second wedding in Rancheria. That ceremony will determine the official date of your union, of course."

Walt snorted. "It may from a legal angle, padre, but as far as I'm concerned, we'll be married from this day forward."

"I'm glad you feel that way, my son. If you did not, I would not agree to officiate."

"Excuse me a moment. I must tell Nastas what's going on."

He hurried out onto the porch, where Nastas was sitting on his heels against the wall. "Nastas, Don Thomas is dying. He's agreed to let me marry Colleen, and we're going to perform the ceremony right now, while he's still able to give her away."

"That is wonderful, *amigo!*" The Navajo beamed with pleasure.

"Yes, but I'm not going to be able to direct the herd when it arrives. Would you please ride to Angel, and ask him to take the herd past the house, and let it into the pastures further up the valley? The horses will be safe there, and the grass is still thick. They can graze for a day or two while we sort all this out. The men should camp near them, to keep them together. Don't let them stray further up the valley into the mountains, the way we came down."

"I will go at once. I wish you joy of your bride."

"Thanks, brother." They clasped hands. "I'll see you and the hands tomorrow."

Walt looked around as Nastas mounted, seeing some of the older workers running towards the house. Clearly, the maid had already passed the word. Half-smiling, he turned towards Don Thomas' bedroom.

Six workers crowded in, forming a line between the foot of the bed and the wall. They all smiled when they saw Walt, and some held out their hands in congratulation. He whispered his thanks as they shuffled back. At the head of the bed, the priest had draped a stole over his shoulders, and was consulting a small book, moving ribbons around to mark places he'd need.

Colleen came in once more, wearing a white dress that buttoned to the neck, topped by a white lace mantilla over her head and shoulders. She looked beautiful. Walt could hardly keep his eyes off her. Margarita followed her into the room, and joined the men at the foot of the bed.

Colleen pressed something into his hand. "Here. This is Mama's wedding ring – she always wanted me to wear it. I've got one of Papa's to put on your finger."

Walt shook his head. "How could I forget about rings? I'm a fool!"

"Hurry!" Don Thomas whispered, coughing. "Please hurry!"

The priest hesitated, then nodded. "I shall leave out most of the liturgy, due to Don Thomas' condition. Let us pray." He turned to a page of his missal and read a prayer in Latin, making the sign of the cross over Walt and Colleen as he did so. The witnesses did likewise, and Don Thomas tried to join them, but his hand just twitched on the bedcover. He no longer had the strength to raise it.

The priest asked, "Who gives this woman to be married to this man?"

Colleen took her father's hand, and Walt took hers, so that Don Thomas' hand rested upon them both. The old man's lips quirked. He was clearly trying to smile. "I do," he whispered.

Padre Francisco led them quickly through the vows of marriage and the exchange of rings, then wrapped his stole around their joined hands. "What God has united, man may not separate. By the authority vested in me by the one, holy, catholic and apostolic Church, I confirm and bless your union in the name of the Father, and of the Son, and of the Holy Spirit, amen. I now pronounce you husband and wife."

Colleen lifted her veil, tears in her eyes as she lifted her face to him. He bent forward and kissed her gently, as the witnesses clapped softly in the background, their eyes alight with joy.

"Thank you, dearest," she whispered as she clung to him. "Thank you so much!"

Before he could answer, Don Thomas coughed explosively, convulsing in bed. A terrible rattle came from his throat as he fell back, breathing hoarsely. *"Papa!"* Colleen cried, whirling around and kneeling by the bed, seizing his hand in hers. The six men and one woman at the foot of the bed craned forward, faces pale with shock and sadness.

Don Thomas coughed twice more, then suddenly jerked bolt upright. His face lit up with joy. He exclaimed, in a loud, hoarse but exultant voice, "Samanta! *Samanta!*"... then he fell back on the pillows and closed his eyes.

His breathing slowed, then stopped.

Colleen looked at her father in awe, then up at Walt. "That was Mama! He *saw* her!"

Padre Francisco said softly, "I have seen that before, *señorita* – I mean, *señora*. Sometimes, not always, when someone dies, one whom they loved greatly seems to appear to them, if we are to judge by their reaction. Holy Mother Church does not pronounce on that matter, but I have always thought it is a sign of the mercy and love of God, to reunite loved ones at such a time. Perhaps He sends them, to take their loved one home to Heaven with them."

Colleen nodded. "Look at his face! He was so *happy!* He hasn't looked like that in years!"

Walt squeezed her hand. "Let's be grateful for that, dearest. He died as happy as a man can be. I know you'll miss him, but you'll always remember him at this moment. Nothing can ever take that away from you. Take comfort in it."

She rose shakily to her feet, and hugged him. "Thank you so much for marrying me like this, Walt! He always said he wanted to give me away at the altar. Well, there's no altar, and he didn't get to give me away in the usual sense, but I think he felt it, anyway."

"I am sure he did," Padre Francisco agreed. "It is customary to bury the dead swiftly. I shall return to Rancheria, and prepare the grave next to your mother's. If you will wash, dress and prepare the body, you can bring it into town tomorrow, and we shall hold a funeral Mass for him. We can solemnize your marriage as well, in the church. I shall prepare the papers for you. Shall we say noon?"

"I'll have everyone there at noon, padre," Walt promised.

"Then I shall leave you for now. Would someone please have my cart brought round?"

"I shall get it, padre," one of the workers promised.

"And I shall summon the women," Margarita said. "We shall prepare him while the men make his coffin. *Señorita,* you were up most of the past three nights. You are very tired. You should rest."

"I must help," Colleen protested.

Walt shook his head. "You've done enough, love, and you're so tired you're shaking. Come on. Let me help you to your bedroom. Margarita, please come with us, and help her undress. I'll leave you to sleep in peace."

"But... what about... us?" She blinked at him.

"We've all the time in the world for that. Rest first, darling."

MARGARITA SHOWED Walt to the same guest room he'd used on his previous visit. He fetched a change of clothing from his saddlebags, then scrubbed off the trail dust and dirt in a hot bath. Refreshed and clean, he ate a light supper.

He looked into Colleen's bedroom after the meal, to find her fast asleep, worn out by the sadness and travail of the previous few days. He kissed the top of her head, tiptoed out, and closed the door.

He'd been vaguely aware of noises from the nearest barn. He walked across to it, and found most of the men of the ranch gathered around a pair of trestles. Across them rested a half-made coffin. Some of the men were sawing planks to size, others were nailing and screwing them together and boring holes for rope handles, and one was standing by with a tin of varnish.

"Good evening, *patrón*," they chorused as they saw him. Walt couldn't understand their use of the term for a moment... then it hit him. He was now Colleen's husband, and as such, by Mexican custom, he was now the custodian of the *estancia* and all who lived there. He had taken Don Thomas' place, and inherited his title.

"Good evening," he replied, a little gruffly. "Is all going well?"

"It is, *patrón*," an older man answered. "I am Virgilio, one of the grooms. Are we all to go to the funeral tomorrow?"

"All of you who wish. I'll ask my men and the guards to keep watch over the *estancia* while we're gone. A few of them can come with us, just in case."

"*Gracias, patrón*. We would not wish Don Thomas to go to his grave without us."

"No, that wouldn't be right. We'll put Don Thomas' body in a wagon tomorrow morning for the ride to Rancheria."

"We shall be ready, *patrón.*"

He walked back to the house, to find Margarita waiting for him. She held a tailor's measuring tape in her hands. "We have prepared Don Thomas for burial, *patrón.* Now we must prepare you for the funeral, and for your church wedding. We, the women of the *estancia,* will alter some of Don Thomas' clothes for you, so you can be properly dressed. He would have wanted that."

The determination in her voice warned him that she would brook no arguments, so he submitted to her measuring him with the tape.

"Thank you, *patrón.* All will be ready in the morning."

13

A small convoy assembled in front of the ranch house next morning. At the head was Caroline's buggy, harnessed to two horses. Walt would ride with her. Behind them came a small buckboard, bearing the coffin with Don Thomas. Behind that was a celerity wagon to carry the *estancia*'s womenfolk. The men would ride in another wagon behind that. Walt arranged for four of the gunhands who'd been protecting the farm to ride into Rancheria with them, including Sergeant Robles, the *Guardia Rural* representative. Even though he wasn't expecting trouble, he told the rest of the guards and his trail hands to be on the alert, just in case.

Margarita surprised him by presenting him with a formal black cutaway jacket, black trousers, a black bow tie, and a frilly-fronted white silk shirt. Don Thomas had been bigger in the body, but all the clothes had been taken in to his measurements. The jacket was still a little large, but the rest fit like they'd been made for him. Feeling awkward, he tried to thank her for the hours of effort she and the other ladies must have put into the clothes, but she waved him off. "It is only fitting that you look the part, *patrón*. Don Thomas will be looking down on us today, along with his wife. They must see that all is as it should be."

He hastily polished his boots, then dressed. He couldn't carry a holstered gun at his waist, in the usual way, for a funeral and wedding. He'd been planning on thrusting one into his waistband, covered by the jacket, but its looser fit offered a way around that. He retrieved another Smith & Wesson Russian Model revolver from his saddlebags. Its barrel had been shortened by a gunsmith in Denver, to make it easier to conceal. He put on its custom-made shoulder holster, inserted the gun, and adjusted holster and jacket so the weapon wasn't visible.

He ate a light breakfast with Colleen, who was wearing the dress she'd donned for their hasty marriage the day before. She hugged him fiercely when she saw him. "Thank you *so much!*" she whispered. "It was so wonderful to have Papa take part in our wedding!"

"We'll have to do it again today, to satisfy the legalities," he reminded her.

She sniffed. "If we must, we must, but I feel as you said yesterday. As far as I'm concerned, we're already married." Her eyes twinkled at him. "In fact, if we weren't already so smartly dressed, I'd suggest we adjourn to my – *our* bedroom, and make up for lost time!"

He had to struggle to suppress an instant surge of arousal. "Soon. Count on it."

"Oh, I am!"

"You're not feeling too sad over your father?"

"I'm sad, yes, and I'm going to miss him very much, but I've known for years that this was coming. It wasn't a surprise. Besides, I've never seen him look like that. He died so joyfully! I hope my death is like that, when my time comes."

"May that time be a long, long way away!"

~

Six of the *estancia* workers served as pallbearers to carry Don Thomas' coffin into the little adobe church at Rancheria. Padre Francisco asked them to set it on trestles just inside the door. "We shall perform your marriage ceremony first," he explained to Walt and Colleen. "It will go quickly, as it is not a nuptial Mass. The Mass today will be offered for Don Thomas. When your wedding is over, we shall move the coffin up to the altar."

Walt noted that the priest had already had a grave dug at one side of the double plot that Don Thomas had bought for himself and his wife. As they waited, he whispered to Colleen, "It's good that he'll be buried here, beside his wife. We can always come back and visit their graves, if you want to; and that'll only get easier, what with the railways expanding everywhere. They'll lie where they lived and died. That seems fitting, somehow."

"Yes," she agreed. "It wouldn't have been right to take him with us, to bury him in Colorado. He never lived there, and it wasn't his home, and Mama wouldn't be there with him."

The second wedding ceremony went off without a hitch. Padre Francisco had them sign the church registry, and issued them with a religious certificate of marriage, plus a secular marriage license issued by the *alcalde*. "I had him prepare this for you this morning," he explained.

"Please thank him for us," Walt replied. "Do we owe anything for his fee?"

"It is ten pesos, *señor.*"

Walt handed over a hundred dollars, in various denominations of gold coins. "Please pay him out of this, Padre, and keep the rest for yourself. It's a thank offering for our wedding and Don Thomas' funeral. Thank you for all you've done for all of us. We're very grateful."

The priest stared at the money for a moment, as if hypnotized. It was probably more money than he earned in a year. He managed to say, "You... you are very generous, *señor.* Thank you."

The funeral mass was long-drawn-out, and mostly in Latin.

Walt had no idea what to do or when to do it. He took his cues from Colleen, and hoped he was not shaming her by his ignorance of Catholic ritual. He occasionally glanced around, to make sure all was well. The four guards stood at the rear of the church, just in case, and the farm workers and their families clustered just behind himself and Colleen in the few simple wooden chairs at the front. Some townspeople who had heard of Don Thomas' passing attended as well, standing in the center of the church in the space behind the chairs.

Colleen held up well until they carried the coffin out to the graveyard next to the church. After more prayers, the pallbearers used ropes to lower the coffin into the pit prepared for it. As it dropped below the surface of the ground, she gave a low cry, and buried her face in Walt's shoulder. He embraced her, supporting her while the ropes were withdrawn. As soon as the final blessing had been given, he led her away gently while two grave-diggers began to fill in the hole.

"What about a headstone?" he asked her.

She blew her nose, wiped her eyes, and looked up. "He already bought one to go at the head of both graves. All the stonemason will need to do is carve the date of his death. Padre Francisco will see to it."

"Indeed I shall," the priest promised as they walked out of the graveyard onto the street. The farmworkers followed them. "When it is done, I shall have a picture taken when the next photographer passes through town. Please leave me your address, so I can send it to you."

"Thank you. I – *Walt!*" She clutched his arm in sudden alarm as six men turned into the street, a block away, and began to walk towards them. "That's Enrique Sandoval! He's the man who's been trying to get his hands on Papa's horses!"

Walt signaled, and the four guards moved forward to stand on either side of him. He assessed the oncoming men coldly. Five were the same sort of men he'd seen at Nueva Rosita, and in the horseshoe canyon, and outside the *estancia*. They were common *pistoleros,* probably just run-of-the-mill, not top-class with their guns. The sixth, however... he was different. Sandoval wore a white shirt, clean and pressed, with a silver-clasped black string tie over black trousers and gleaming boots. His gun, which looked like a nickel-plated 1860 Army Colt from this distance, bore solid silver Tiffany-style grips, glinting in the sunlight. He carried it in an ornately carved and embellished black leather holster with silver metal trim. His waistcoat, black embroidered with silver braid, was tailored to give his hand free access to the weapon.

Walt thought fast as he gently pulled free from Colleen's embrace and motioned her to one side, out of the line of fire. *That's a real fancy gun and holster. If he knows how to use them, he'll draw faster than I can from a shoulder holster... unless I can trick him.*

He frowned suddenly as six of the *estancia* workers moved forward to flank the guards. He opened his mouth to order them back, then blinked in surprise as they pulled back their jackets, revealing revolvers thrust into their waistbands, just as Walt had first planned to wear his today. The six oncoming men suddenly hesitated, uncertainty clouding their faces. Instead of odds of six to five in their favor, they now faced eleven to six – a rather less attractive proposition.

"Who the hell are those *campesinos* pretending to be *pistoleros?*" Sandoval called arrogantly.

"You lost six *pistoleros* a few weeks ago, remember?" Colleen taunted from where she stood with Padre Francisco. "They met up with my husband. He brought their guns back to the *estancia*. I had our guards teach six of my men how to use them. They've been practising. Judging by those you lost, by now they're probably as good as or better than your men."

Walt called, grinning, "Colleen, that was a great idea! I'm proud of you! What do you want, *Señor* Sandoval?"

"You must be that arrogant *gringo* who thinks he's going to steal my horses."

"I bought all Don Thomas' horses a month ago, and paid for them. They're not yours, they never were, and they never will be."

"You'll never leave here with them."

"On the contrary. I'm taking them, and my wife, and all the *estancia*'s workers, to America with me, and there's not a damned thing you can do about it."

"My men will shoot you from ambush, stampede your horses with bush fires, and block your trail with fallen trees and rocks. You won't make it to the border unless you give me the horses now, and sign over the *estancia* to me. If you do, I'll let you leave with no trouble."

"No deal. What's more, *señor* Sandoval, you've just threatened my wife's safety and property, as well as mine." He half-turned his head. "Sergeant Robles, would the *Guardia Rural* agree I have the right to defend my wife against those threats?"

"Of course, *señor* – not only the right, but the duty. That is entirely within the law."

For the first time, Sandoval looked uncertain. "You brought the *Guardia* here?"

"Just me," Robles retorted with a mocking smile, "but one of us is enough, no?"

"Thank you, Sergeant." Walt ostentatiously unbuttoned his jacket and smoothed it over his hips, trying to give the impression it concealed a gun thrust into his waistband, just like those the *campesinos* from the *estancia* were displaying. He looked beyond Sandoval to the five *pistoleros* standing behind him. "You men can back Sandoval's play, and die with him, or you can drop your guns, turn around, and walk away. You have ten seconds to decide."

"*Nobody moves!*" Sandoval screeched, fury in his eyes. "You cannot do this!"

"Try me," Walt invited flatly.

One of the men behind Sandoval licked his suddenly dry lips. The odds no longer suited him. He'd known some of the six *pistoleros* who had not returned, a month ago. If this *gringo* had, indeed, killed them all, he was too good with a gun to take a chance – particularly with ten armed men supporting him, one of them a *Guardia* sergeant.

"I'm out," he said thickly. With finger and thumb he slowly lifted his revolver from its holster, bent, and laid it in the dust of the street; then he took two steps backward, turned, and scurried away. Within seconds, another did likewise. The three remaining *pistoleros* hesitated, uncertainty in their faces; but they stood their ground.

"Sandoval's mine," Walt warned his people without turning around. "The four guards take the other three men. Everyone else, including the *estancia* workers, get out of the way."

Within seconds, Colleen called from the church gate, "They're all out of the line of fire." Her voice trembled a little.

Walt raised his arms and crossed them, trying to appear deliberately casual. He knew the implied insult – that he believed he could beat Sandoval to the draw even from so slow and awkward a starting position – would enrage the man even further. Beneath his crossed arms, Walt's right hand crept into the left side of his jacket, closing on the grip of his revolver in its shoulder holster. That was half his draw stroke completed already, before the fight had even begun.

"When you're ready, *Señor* Sandoval," he invited.

Sandoval hesitated a moment; then he screamed *"Hijo de puta!"* and grabbed for his gun.

He was as fast as Walt had expected, but he had to start his draw from the beginning. Walt didn't. His right hand whipped out of his jacket, the hammer on the Smith and Wesson coming back under his thumb as he snapped out his arm at full extension. His finger twitched on the tuned trigger. A two-hundred-

and-forty-six grain, .44 caliber lead bullet churned through the rifling and out of the muzzle.

Sandoval drew his gun with lightning speed, but Walt's bullet slammed into him before he could line it. He grunted aloud and staggered, pain and fear etched on his face, but he still held his revolver. Walt didn't hesitate. Dimly aware of guns thundering on either side of him, he triggered three more rounds, sending them into a tight cluster with the first in Sandoval's chest, over his heart. The man stumbled back, his white shirt turning red with his life's blood. He dropped his weapon, then crumpled to the ground.

Walt took a deep breath, looking at the three *pistoleros* who'd backed their boss. All were down. One had part of his head torn away, blood and gray brain matter leaking out. Another was face-down, unmoving, the back of his shirt torn and bloody where slugs had burst through. The third was on the ground, supporting himself on one elbow, coughing up blood, proof that at least one bullet had pierced his lungs.

Walt glanced to either side. One of the four guards was holding his left arm and cursing, blood showing through his fingers, but none of the others appeared to be hurt. That wasn't surprising, of course; they'd been selected for their handiness with their guns, which was better than the average *bandido*. Walt holstered his gun and walked over to the wounded man. He gently prised his fingers open, and exhaled with relief. "It's all right. The bullet just creased you. We'll clean and bandage it, and you'll be fine within a couple of weeks. No real harm done."

"Thank you, *señor*," the other said, a baleful gleam in his eye. "That *cabron* got lucky. I hit him before he hit me, but he lasted just long enough to do this."

"It could have been worse. Be grateful for that."

"*Walt!*" Colleen ran into his arms, hugging him fiercely. "Are you all right?"

"Not a scratch on me, darling." He bent and kissed her. "I'm sorry you had to see that. Don't worry. It's over."

"Oh, never mind seeing that! After all the trouble he caused for us, I'm glad he's dead! I was just scared I might become a widow almost as soon as I'd become a wife. Things can always go wrong, can't they?"

"That's true enough. Today, thanks be to God, they didn't – at least, not for us. They sure did for Sandoval, though." He turned to Sergeant Robles. "Is there anything you want me to do, Sergeant?"

"No, *señor*. As I said, you had the right to act as you did. I shall report to the *Comandante* that you acted entirely within the law, and have no case to answer. Besides," and he laughed unpleasantly, "you've saved me the trouble of having to give them *ley fuga* on the way back to the prison at Monclova."

"Thank you, sergeant, particularly for your assistance back there. I think I owe you a bonus, over and above the fee the *Comandante* said I should pay you."

"You are generous, *señor*. I thank you. I shall take charge of these *bandidos'* guns, and the contents of their pockets, to hand in at Monclova."

Walt guessed that anything valuable, particularly the silver-handled Colt, would never make it that far, but he didn't care. Colleen clearly felt differently. She asked, "May I keep Sandoval's gun and holster? They'll be a reminder of his threats, and my husband's bravery. I'll make a contribution to the *Guardia* to cover their cost, if you wish."

"Of course you may, *señora*. I will bring them to you."

Colleen turned to Walt. "How did you think up that trick, folding your arms to hide reaching for your gun? I've never heard of that before."

"I used it once before, when dealing with a pack of outlaws in Missouri just after the war. It was a spur-of-the-moment thing then, but I remembered it, figurin' it might come in useful again sometime. Sure enough, it just did." He turned to Padre Francisco. "Padre, will you give these men decent burial?"

"I shall, my son. What of the six others your wife mentioned?"

"We buried them on the range, about a mile from the *estancia*. There is no marker. Look for a bare heap of earth near the trail. I don't know their names."

"I shall go out there and bless the grave. They doubtless had more need of grace and mercy than most."

"Thank you." Walt reached for his wallet, and handed over another fifty dollars. "This will pay for four more graves, and for the extra work I've made for you. We're grateful." He turned to Colleen. "Shall we go home, darling?"

"It'll be home only for another day or so, but yes, please!"

THEY STEPPED out onto the porch. The twilight had faded, the stars had come out, and a half-moon was shining in the night sky. They stood silently, looking around without speaking, for a minute or two.

"I'm sure you'll miss this place," Walt said. "What will you do with it? I mean, it's yours now, isn't it?"

"Yes, but it's complicated. Papa owned the land on which this house and the other buildings stand. All the rest – the pastures, the outlying corrals, and so on – are on open range. We're using them because we got here first, but that doesn't mean someone else couldn't buy them, or take them away from us. A lot of *estancias* are like that. I could try to sell this place, but it'll take a year or more for Papa's will to be probated and the property put into my name. That would mean I'd have to stay here, to deal with lawyers and courts, and you'd have to leave without me. Even after the legal process was over, finding a buyer would be very difficult."

She sighed. "The French occupation messed up this country

terribly, and it's going to take years for its effects to wear off. Mexico's politics are in chaos. Many governors obey the President only if it suits them. The Army's riven by factions, with generals setting themselves up as local warlords. Many who fought for or against the French have gone into business for themselves, as *bandidos* or *pistoleros*. Sandoval was one of them. He's dead now, but someone will take his place before long. There's no stability any more. It's not safe to stay. Papa planned to just walk away from here, so that's what I'll do. You made that possible, of course – you paid much more for our horses than we'd have got by selling this place."

"I'm sorry. I wish there was something I could do to help you keep it."

She smiled up at him, teeth gleaming against her lips. "You've done something better. You've married me, and you're taking me to my new home with you."

He bent and kissed her upturned mouth. Colleen responded eagerly, reaching up to wrap her arms around his neck, pulling him down to her. The kiss began slowly, but gained intensity by the moment, until they were both breathing hard, savoring the taste of each other's lips and the urgent pressure of their bodies against each other.

"Darling," she said throatily, softly, almost purring, "I... I don't want to go for a walk any more. I want you to take me back to our room."

He scooped her into his arms and carried her back through the door, kicking it closed with his boot as they crossed the threshold. He walked down the hall to her room, pushed open the door and set her down inside, then turned to close it. His head was awhirl with passion.

She stretched, raising her hands high above her head, and smiled at him. "Would my husband care to undress me?" she asked coquettishly.

He reached for the top button of her dress. "Your wish is my command."

LATER, much later, that night, she sighed sleepily. "My *husband...* that word has such a nice sound!"

"And you're my wife. Happy?"

"*Silly!* Of course I am!" She thought for a moment. "You know, I've heard the words 'husband' and 'wife' many times, but I never really knew what they meant before tonight. I'm yours now, *truly* yours, in a way I could never properly understand before."

"That goes both ways, darling."

They snuggled into each others' arms, and drifted off to sleep.

14

They stayed one more day at the *estancia*. Colleen supervised the last of the packing, and double-checked that everything important had been loaded, including all the food. Walt paid off the gunhands from Monclova, including a hundred-dollar bonus to Sergeant Robles, who thanked him effusively. He then supervised his men in branding the *estancia's* horses with his Rafter A brand, lightly underlined twice to distinguish the breeding stock from the less valuable animals. They were then driven into the herd from Saltillo and allowed to mingle with them.

"D'you reckon we have enough men to handle over six hundred horses?" he asked Angel.

"Yes, *señor*. The horses from Saltillo are all accustomed to the rope, and know not to fight it, so they stay inside our simple rope corral at night on the trail. Those from the *estancia* may not, but they will learn from the example of the others. We may have to rope a few of them if they break out, but that will teach the rest not to do that."

"Fair enough. Let's try, and see how they take it."

"*Si, señor.*"

Four of the hands took long ropes from pack horses, and strung them at chest height around bushes and trees to form a circle, with an opening left at one end. The herd was driven into the rope circle. Most of the horses had been repeatedly lassoed in the past. They understood the futility of fighting a rope, and so regarded the makeshift corral as a much stronger containment than it really was. However, the *estancia's* horses had been treated with greater delicacy, and had not yet developed as much caution where ropes were concerned.

One of the *estancia's* stallions showed that he had no intention of being confined inside something so flimsy as a rope corral by these two-legged creatures. He broke back the first time the horses were driven into it, and jumped over the rope the second time. On each occasion, the hands chased him down, and drove him back to the corral.

Walt turned to Angel. "He's got to be stopped. That sort of behavior's catching. Next time he tries, teach him a lesson."

"*Si, señor.*" The *mesteñero* took his lariat off his saddlehorn and spread out the loop, ready for action.

Sure enough, the next time the rope corral was moved and the herd driven in, the stallion broke back again, galloping away from the mouth of the corral, heading for the open range. Angel spurred his horse after him, accelerating fast before the stallion could get away. He began to whirl the lariat over his head, building its momentum, then sent it sailing out. It crossed over the shoulder of the blithely unaware stallion, then a twitch of Angel's wrist sent it downward. It hit the horse's knees, then dropped further to catch its forefeet in the loop. Angel pulled back on the rope, and the horse's front legs locked together abruptly. It crashed to the ground, neighing shrilly in fear and outrage. Its calls were cut off as the breath was slammed from its body.

Walt nodded approvingly. The forefoot throw had been beautifully executed by a master of the craft. There was a risk that the stallion might have broken its neck, but better that than have it ruin other animals by teaching them its habit of disobedience. They could not afford to keep chasing after horses, particularly when they reached Indian territory. There, a rider pursuing an escaping horse might find a lot more trouble than he'd bargained for.

He watched as Angel got off his horse and removed the loop. The stallion staggered to its feet, then rejoined the herd with no further urging. This time, it did not attempt to break back or jump over the rope.

"Well done, Angel," Walt praised as the *mesteñero* rejoined him, coiling his rope. "Reckon he's learned his lesson?"

"I hope so, *señor*. If he has not, we shall have to repeat it."

"If need be, go right ahead. On my ranch, with plenty of time to use gentle methods, I'm all for them; but we have to hit the trail, and we've run out of time. He's got to learn fast. If that means the hard way, well..."

Both men shrugged.

THAT NIGHT, Walt asked one of the workers to cut him four pieces of wood, each a foot square and two inches deep, with a notch cut in the center of two sides, opposite each other. The man delivered the sawed and sanded pieces to him within an hour.

"What are those for?" Colleen asked, puzzled, when he showed her.

Walt grinned. "I'll show you."

He took her out to her parents' converted celerity wagon, now a comfortable canvas-sided camping wagon, with room to store personal possessions, food, and the like. "We want to sleep in this, don't we?"

"Yes, of course. I want my husband in my bed at night!"

"And he wants to be there, but..." Instead of saying more, Walt reached out and pressed down on the rear corner of the wagon bed, bouncing it gently on its elliptical springs. They creaked in the still night air. He kept on bouncing the wagon bed, and Colleen blushed scarlet as she suddenly realized what he meant.

"*Oh!* I never thought of that!"

"That's what these blocks of wood are for." He slid them in between the springs at each corner of the wagon bed, lifting it slightly to make room for them. The notches held them in place between the top and bottom springs, preventing them from contracting. When he tried to bounce the wagon bed again, it didn't move. More importantly, the springs didn't creak.

Colleen burst out laughing. "How did you think of that?"

Walt grinned. "Rose and I had the same problem in the Rucker ambulance I converted for her, when we came west across Missouri, Kansas and Colorado. I learned that trick from an Army private who taught us how to handle six-mule teams. You put them in when you stop for the night, and take them out in the morning. Good thing I remembered before we left."

"I'm glad you did. I want your company, darling – but without the whole world knowing about it!"

THE NEXT DAY, they hit the trail at sunrise. Walt rode his horse, and Colleen drove her buggy. "I'll work up to riding all day, too," she promised, "but let me start slowly."

"No problem, as long as there's a trail. When that runs out, I don't know whether your buggy will be able to cope."

"You're probably right, but I'll use it as long as I can."

Walt stopped the herd for the night outside Nueva Rosita. He invited Colleen and a couple of the *estancia*'s women to come into town with him as the sun set. She and Walt rode in her buggy, while the others drove a light wagon.

Walt led them to the house occupied by young Maria, her

mother, and her grandfather. They looked astonished to see him
again – this time with a retinue. He grinned at them as he introduced his wife and the women. "May we come in?" he asked. "I
have much to tell you."

When they had crowded into the small front room, Walt told
the family about what he'd read in the diary, and what he'd done
about it. He didn't go into detail about the money, but described
how following Major d'Assaily's route had led him to the *estancia,*
where he'd met and married Colleen and bought her father's
entire horse herd. "I owe all that to you," he finished. "I wanted to
thank you for giving me the diary, and for your prayers for me
each night. They've led to my being married once more, and
going home rich in love, in horses, and in money."

The old man smiled. "It is good to know God has used us to
bless you, *señor.*"

"He certainly has. I'm willing to give you a lot of money as a
reward for all you did to help me, but I don't know how safe that
would be. I remember those *bandidos* who tried to make trouble.
I'm sure they're not the only ones of that kind you've seen here. If
they heard you had money, they might try to steal it from you."

Edelmira shivered. "They would not just rob us, *señor.* They
would torture us to make sure they had found all the money, then
they would kill us." Her father nodded silently.

"That's what I feared, so I have another offer for you. I'm
taking the *estancia*'s workers back to America with me, to my
horse ranch in Colorado. I'll build them houses there. They'll
work for me, and I'll pay them each month, and they can stay in
their houses even after their working years, if they wish. I'm
willing to make you the same offer. We can load your belongings
onto the wagon outside, and you can travel with us. I'll help you
find work on the ranch or in Pueblo, and we'll put Maria into
school."

"School?" Her mother's voice was suddenly excited. "She will
learn to read and write?"

"She sure will, and more besides. There are classes for adults, too. You could do the same."

Walt asked Colleen and the two women to reassure Edelmira that his offer was genuine. She listened in fascination as they described packing up everything in the *estancia,* and their departure. It didn't take long to convince her that Walt was serious.

The old man wavered. *"Señor,* I am not the man I used to be. I do not think I could work hard enough to earn my wages."

"You've already earned them, Guillermo. You gave me that diary, which led me to my new wife and everything else. You don't need to do anything more for me, ever again."

A smile dawned on the old man's face, and his eyes lit up. "Edelmira?"

"I... do you think this is right for us, papa?"

"Yes. Yes, I do. I think this is an opportunity that comes once in a lifetime. What is more, we will not be alone in a strange place among strangers. Many of our own people will move there with us, like these two ladies." He nodded towards the women from the *estancia.*

Edelmira took a deep breath. "Come, Maria. Let us pack your clothes. We are going to Colorado!" Her daughter squealed with delight.

There wasn't much to pack. They had very little furniture and not many clothes. It took no more than half an hour to load the wagon with their pitifully few possessions.

The old man came out of the house and closed the door behind him, then handed Walt the gray kepi. "I think you should take this now, *señor,* and put it with the other things. It is fitting that they should remain together."

"I will. Thank you."

Back at the campsite, Colleen supervised the preparing of food and sleeping spaces for the new additions to their number. Meanwhile, Walt sought out Nastas. "You remember the horseshoe canyon where we dealt with those three *bandidos?*" he asked.

"Yes, very well."

"You remember the rock under which the old man buried the soldier? The one marked with a cross scratched on it?"

"Yes, that too."

"The man buried there was a warrior as well as a soldier. He fought bravely until he was too wounded to fight on, and even then took steps to help his friends continue his mission, if they found him. He never fought alongside me, but we wore the same uniform. I don't want to leave him there, forgotten. I'd like to bring his bones back with us, to send them to his family for honorable burial."

"An excellent thought. A warrior should be honored by his people."

"Will you help me do that? I can't go back to that valley myself – I've got to see to the herd and everyone with us – but if you're willing, I'll ask you to go there and dig up his remains. He was buried more than eight years ago, without a coffin, so his body's sure to have decayed. There'll only be bones left, and maybe some scraps of his uniform. If you'll put them into a pack horse pannier and bring them back to the herd, I'll buy a small box to hold them for the journey to Colorado. Once we get there, I'll see about tracing his family, so they can bury him properly."

Nastas nodded. "Of course. I shall leave at dawn. How long will you be on the trail from here to the border?"

"Four days, I think."

"Then that is easy. I shall rejoin you before you get there."

Walt shook his hand in real gratitude. "Thanks, Nastas. I owe you for this."

The Navajo shook his head vehemently. "No, you do not. This is a service I, a warrior, can render to a fallen warrior. Because he wore the same uniform as you, he counts as your ally, and therefore mine, too. It is an honor for me to do this. Nothing is owed."

Nastas was as good as his word. The night before reaching Piedras Negras, he rode into the camp, leading his pack horse. He dismounted, took a pannier from the pack saddle, and carried it over to Walt. "Here are your brother's bones," he said solemnly. "I made sure to gather them all, leaving none behind. I have handled them with honor, as I would want mine to be treated if I were in his place."

Walt took them from him. "Thanks, Nastas. I'll take good care of them from now on."

He put the pannier into a wood box that he'd bought before leaving Nueva Rosita. Major d'Assaily's mortal remains would be safe there for the rest of the journey.

CROSSING the border proved to be easier than Walt had expected. He'd been worried that getting the *estancia* workers into America might be difficult, particularly since none of them had travel documents. However, passage of workers across the border in both directions was so common that no questions were asked. Since the horses were being brought into the country to meet Army requirements, and he had a letter to prove that, no import duty was payable. He carefully failed to mention his own horses that were mixed in with the Army's mounts.

Walt paused for the rest of the day on the American side, in the town of Eagle Pass, to catch up on minor details. He telegraphed Pablo in El Paso, asking him to send an update to Fort Clark on how things had gone, and Nate on the ranch, advising him of the arrival in a few months of his new wife, plus a couple of dozen *estancia* workers and their families.

The workers' clothing was proving less than adequate for the rigors of living out of a wagon on the trail for weeks on end. Walt sent a telegraph message to a supplier in San Antonio, recommended by a local storekeeper, asking for a selection of tough readymade clothing, bolts of suitable cloth, sewing thread, needles and other necessities to be sent to Fort Clark. He also ordered a large quantity of supplies, for the journey north to El Paso and beyond. He knew the sutler at Fort Clark would be unable to provide all he needed. Meanwhile, he almost cleaned out the stocks of the general store in Eagle Pass. When that wasn't enough, he sent a wagon back across the border to buy more in Piedras Negras.

Their arrival at the fort, two days later, was cause for celebration. Tyler Reese and his men were already there, waiting for them. Walt paid off the hands he'd hired in Mexico and sent them on their way, smiling in satisfaction as they counted their gold dollars. He had his ranch hands separate his breeding stock from the rest of the herd. They amounted to two hundred and seventeen horses, both from the *estancia* and the best of those bought in Saltillo and Monterrey. The rest, less the wagon teams and working horses, were inspected, passed as suitable, and formally accepted by the cavalry.

Colonel Mackenzie looked over the horses, and pronounced himself satisfied. "You've done all I asked of you, and more. General Sheridan agreed with my request, and increased our horse-buying budget. Like me, he thinks this year will see hard fighting to contain the Comanche and Kiowa, and he wants the cavalry prepared for trouble. Come to my office, and I'll give you a U.S. government draft to cover all your horses."

Walt invited Tyler to accompany him, since he'd invested three thousand dollars of his own money in their venture. They sat down and tallied up the numbers. Between the two of them, they'd delivered 2,107 horses to Fort Clark, bought for an average of almost exactly $8 per head, including local labor and feed costs averaged across the herd. The horses had been sold to the Army for a pre-contracted price of $25 each. Tyler had bought 375 of those horses with his money, so he received a draft for $9,375. Walt had bought the rest, using his own funds and part of those he'd recovered from Major d'Assaily's cache. That brought him a draft for $43,300.

Even though he'd known the return on his investment would be good if everything went as it should, Walt was still staggered at the amount of the draft in his hand. He said so, and Colonel Mackenzie smiled. "Don't forget the horses your partner's delivered in El Paso," he reminded him. "They'll bring in more money."

"I asked him to send me a report on how he was doing. It should be waiting for me here."

"My adjutant is holding a telegraph message for you. Check with him as you go out."

"I will, thank you, Colonel."

The senior officer sat back in his chair, looking quizzically at Walt. "You've acquired quite a reputation, and it's spreading fast. People are talking about you, not just in Mexico but in Texas, too."

Walt flushed slightly. "Oh? How's that, sir?"

"Enrique Sandoval may have been bad clear through, but he was a *pistolero* to be reckoned with. People who know what they're talking about, on both sides of the border, say he was the fastest gun in north-eastern Mexico. He ran roughshod over much of Coahuila province for years. His *bandidos* even raided on this side of the Rio Grande from time to time. You made a lot of people very happy when you killed him, and made a name for yourself too. You were already known as a dead shot with a rifle, after the Hunting Wolf incident back in '66, but not so much as a fast gun. I daresay that'll change from now on."

Walt shrugged. "I wouldn't call myself a real fast gun, sir – just fast enough when it's counted, so far. If I never have to pull a revolver in anger again, I won't complain. I'd rather live a peaceful life."

"So would any man with sense. Sadly, there are always bad men who need stopping, and good men have to bestir themselves to do so from time to time. How many of Sandoval's *bandidos* went down with him?"

"Three on the day he died, sir, and at least nine that I know of before then, in a couple of other fights. Tyler, how many did your *segundo* deal with while we were buying horses?"

"Tom told me his gunhands got several more. Only two bodies were left behind – the rest skedaddled on horseback, helping some of their friends to stay astride."

Mackenzie grunted. "With any luck, the wounded will have died later. That'll have thinned the worst of the *bandido* herd there for a while."

"Someone else will take Sandoval's place soon enough, Colonel," Walt pointed out.

"Perhaps, but they'll remember what happened to him, and be more cautious, I think."

Tyler chuckled. "They're likely to think twice before trying to push around unknown *gringos,* anyway."

Mackenzie laughed. "If they have any sense, yes." He pushed back his chair and rose to his feet. "Now, I have to get these horses distributed to the other forts along the frontier. That's going to be a big job. It's early April, and spring's well under way, so at least there'll be good grazing along the trails to the forts; but early Indian raiding and hunting parties will also be out. That means I have to provide bigger escorts for the horse herds, and get them back here when they've delivered them, all while keeping up our regular patrols." He came around the desk. "Thank you again for all you've done. You may be hearing from me soon about the services of your Navajo scouts." He held out his hand.

Walt shook it. "I'll look forward to that, sir."

He collected the telegraph message from the adjutant, noting that it was, indeed, from Pablo, but did not read it at once. Instead, he asked for directions to the fort's ordnance section. There, he explained to the senior NCO about Don Thomas' 1841 pack howitzer, and asked, "Is there any way I can buy more shells for it from you? I don't need powder – I can buy that anywhere – but the shells are a problem."

The sergeant thought for a moment. "Luckily, we just received a shipment to replenish our stocks. A battery is due to conduct training next Monday. If you'll still be here, sir, I can issue them, at least on paper, more rounds than they're due to fire. I can write off the extras as 'consumed during training'. If you and I make a private arrangement, I'll see to it that they're 'consumed' in your direction, if you know what I mean. There are four types of projectile. Shall we say a dozen of each?"

Walt grinned. "That would be fine, sergeant. If you can spare two or three dozen of the solid shot, that would be even better."

After a short negotiation, a price in gold dollars was agreed, payable privately on delivery. Walt rode back to the wagons, whistling cheerfully. There had been no room in the fort for them this time, so they'd pitched camp a mile away, on good grazing for the horses. He sat down with paper and pencil to do some figuring.

Pablo reported that he'd received 1,214 horses from the teams that had gone to central and western Mexico. They'd cost an average of $7.40 apiece. He'd held back 173 for Walt's breeding stock, and delivered 1,041 to Fort Bliss, duly accepted by the Army. He was holding U.S. government drafts totaling $26,025, which he'd hand over when they next met.

Walt added up the numbers. Pablo had invested $2,000 of his own money in this venture, so he'd get $6,756. Vicente had invested $1,000, which he'd sent into Mexico with one of Pablo's teams, so he'd receive $3,378. Walt would get the balance of $15,891. Added to what Colonel Mackenzie had just paid him, his total income from this venture would amount to almost $60,000, payable in gold dollars or the equivalent value in greenbacks. He still owed almost $5,000 in outstanding wages and bonuses, but even so, that left $54,000. He also had another $15,000 or so in cash, courtesy of the late Major d'Assaily, bringing his total to almost $70,000; and Colleen had over $9,000 that he'd paid her father for his horses, bringing the combined total close to $80,000.

Walt was staggered. He'd had to cover initial costs, salaries, and the purchase of the horses, but even so, this was a far larger return than he'd expected. He did some calculations. All told, he'd invested $25,000 of his own money, plus about $20,000 of the gold he'd recovered in Mexico. That gave him a cash return on investment of no less than 40%, plus several hundred horses for his breeding stock – some of them among the finest of their kind he'd ever seen – and some very experienced hands to help breed and train them. He'd also bought a dozen six-mule wagons and their teams, to be transferred to Ames Transport when they got back to Colorado. The Army profits alone would cover everything he'd spent last year on setting up his horse ranch, with several thousand dollars to spare. Last but not least, he'd returned with a wife whom he loved more with every passing day, and who filled him with happiness.

When he showed her the figures, later that evening, Colleen was amazed. "I don't think I've ever seen numbers that big before," she exclaimed. "And it's all yours?"

"Ours, honey."

"*Whew!* I knew you were pretty successful, what with your transport company and your own horse ranch, but this is... it's *wonderful!* Of course, there's also the money you paid Papa for his horses. Now that we're married, I'll return that to you. We'll pool our resources together."

"Are you sure, darling? I don't mind if you want to keep it separate."

She shook her head. "If I need money, I'll ask you, just as I know you'll tell me if you take out a big sum for your own use."

"Sure. That's part of being honest with each other. I want you to draw a monthly allowance, as much as you think you'll need, for your own use – clothes, books and anything else. I'll do the same."

"Let's do that." She looked at him curiously. "How much do you think you're worth now?"

"It's not me, sweetheart. It's 'we'. Rose and I always saw it that way, and I want you to do the same. Let's see... in cash, and adding the value of the land, animals, wagons and buildings of the transport company, and the same for the ranch, and the two farms..."

"Two farms? What two farms?"

"Oh, didn't I tell you? I have a farm of one-and-a-half sections near Salida, and another on two sections of riverfront land near Cañon City. I have tenant farmers on both. I buy animal feed from them – alfalfa and oats. My wagons collect sacks and bales of it whenever they pass. The farmers don't have to pay shipping costs, so it works out cheaper than buying from feed barns."

He'd taken over both farms from Parsons after he'd killed him. He wouldn't tell Colleen about the three small parcels of land in New Mexico yet, he decided. Parsons had invested in them, in the expectation that they lay on the most suitable route for a proposed southern transcontinental railway line, running through Glorieta Pass to Santa Fe. They weren't worth anything to speak of right now, but if Parsons' informants had been correct, that would change overnight once the new railroad's route was announced.

Colleen nodded. "All right. What's the total?"

"All of my properties and businesses are debt-free, so including the money for your father's horses, I'd say we're worth somewhere north of a hundred and forty thousand dollars, cash, land and assets, free and clear."

She stared at him, mouth open in astonishment. She couldn't speak for some moments. When she recovered her voice, she said accusingly, "Why didn't you tell me you were so rich?"

Walt shook his head. "We're comfortably off, but truly rich men, like some of the mine owners in Colorado or the railroad magnates, are worth millions. Also, a single disaster can wipe out a lot of what we own. That's one reason I'm spreadin' it out. If a flood or fire destroys the horse ranch, we'll have the transport company. If the railroads expand so much that the transport company goes under, we'll have the ranch and the farms. I'll invest in other things, too, when I have the time and money to do so."

"You're not putting all our eggs in one basket, as they say. Back in Mexico, you mentioned investing in a cattle ranch."

"Yes. You met Tyler Reese today. He wants to buy land in the Texas Panhandle area as soon as the Indian threat is lifted. He's got some of what he'll need, but not enough. I'm thinking about puttin' in the rest, and becomin' his partner. I don't know how long the Texas beef market's gonna stay healthy. A lot o' herds are being driven to ranches in Nebraska and further north right now. They'll compete to sell to Eastern states once they're up an' runnin'. Even so, I reckon ranching'll stay profitable for a good while longer. I'll invest for ten years, then sell out an' take my profits, and I'll draw an income from the ranch each year as well.

"I'm also lookin' at a property further up the Wet Mountain Valley, north of my ranch. It's about two thousand acres – a bit over three square miles – but half o' that's in the foothills, so it can't be used for much 'cept grazin' or timber. I've got more'n ten thousand acres already, so I don't need it, but the owner wants to sell, and he's offerin' a good price. With what I've earned from this venture, I can easily afford it; and land's not gonna get any cheaper, 'specially big pieces like that. If it ain't been sold by the time we get back, I'll talk to him."

"Does it adjoin your ranch?"

"Naw, it's near on twenty miles above our northern boundary, on the western edge of the Wet Mountains. That ain't a problem, though. We can drive horses there an' back if need be."

Later that night, lying in bed, Walt kissed her gently. "You know, honey, all that money's all very well; but if I lost every penny I brought to this venture, and I'd never found that gold or bought your father's horse herd, I'd still reckon myself rich for finding you."

She blinked back tears as she stroked his cheek. "And I'm richer than I ever thought I'd be, because I've found you."

"Care to find me again?"

She giggled. "I thought you'd never ask!"

THE SHIPMENT of cloth and sewing materials arrived from San Antonio three days later. They held a choosing contest for the ready-made clothes, with much giggling and carrying on as the items were held against bodies and measured by eye. Walt borrowed a room in Fort Clark for the ladies to get to work, altering the ready-mades and making new clothes for the long, laborious journey to El Paso, Fort Union and Colorado.

Colleen learned that a couple of the fort's wives owned treadle-powered sewing machines. She prevailed on Walt to hire them, and the services of their owners, for a few days. It made the sewing and alterations much quicker; but of greater interest was that Edelmira displayed an innate gift for working the machines fast, accurately and neatly. Walt examined some cotton bib shirts she'd run up for him, and was impressed.

"Maybe we should buy a sewing machine for the ranch, and set her up there to make clothes for everyone," he suggested to Colleen.

She shook her head. "She'll be wasted there. Why not set her up in business in Pueblo? It'll be closer to good schools for Maria, and she can make a good living at it. She can teach the ranch women how to use a sewing machine, and we can buy one or two for them."

"All right. We'll do that."

"What about Sancho? He's been spending a lot of time with her lately. I think there may be wedding bells in due course."

They'd been watching the budding romance with amusement. Both Sancho and Edelmira had been married before, but their former partners had died. Their pleasure in each other was obvious, and even better, Maria doted on her prospective stepfather. What's more, Guillermo approved of him.

Walt grinned. "He works out at the ranch, but if he marries her, I can just as easily use him in the transport company, at the same wage. I reckon he won't mind moving to Pueblo to be with her."

The freight wagons also brought copies of the latest newspapers from San Antonio. Walt's defeat of Enrique Sandoval had made minor headline news. He read the reports with growing irritation. The journalists who had written them appeared to favor breathless hyperbole over facts. He crumpled up one newspaper and threw it into the fire, letting out an oath of frustration.

"Damned hacks! It wasn't anything like that!"

Colleen leaned over and hugged him. "Never mind, darling. Didn't Colonel Mackenzie say Sandoval had been feared in these parts for some time? I suppose his death was bound to catch their imagination."

"Yeah, but the way they wrote about it, you'd think I was some sort of angel of death, sent to pass judgment on Sandoval for his sins!" Walt stared moodily at the flames flaring up as they began to consume the newsprint sheets.

She giggled. "Never mind. The important thing is, we're alive and unhurt, and have the rest of our lives ahead of us. Sandoval doesn't."

Walt shook his head. "You don't understand, love. Some men – not many, thank God! – think it's some sort of game to see who's the fastest gun out there. Some of them will travel long distances to meet someone they think they can beat, and force him into a gunfight. If they kill him, they reckon it'll add to their reputation. Others of that sort won't fight themselves, but take bets on those who do. I don't want anyone to start thinking of me as a likely target."

She sobered at once. "I didn't know that! What sort of diseased mind works that way?"

"I don't know, sweetheart, and I hope to God I never find out for myself. I just want to keep a low profile, stay out of the limelight, and get on with the business of living."

She shivered. "We'll have to add that to our prayers, and hope that such people don't read the San Antonio newspapers."

Over the next three days, everyone received the fruits of the ladies' labor; ample supplies of new clothing, sufficiently tough to stand up to two more months on the trail. The supplies were distributed among the wagons and pack horses. Harness, saddles and tack were overhauled and prepared, and those horses that needed it were re-shoed. Walt asked Colonel Mackenzie for an escort, and the Colonel obliged with half a platoon, ten cavalry troopers commanded by a sergeant. He apologized for not sending more men, but what with having to distribute among several forts all the horses Walt had brought, he simply couldn't spare them.

Walt's private arrangement with the ordnance sergeant also bore fruit. Sixty rounds for the mountain howitzer – two dozen cannonballs, and a dozen each of case shot, canister and grapeshot – were carefully stowed, in exchange for five twenty-dollar double-eagle coins.

At last, all was ready. Fifteen wagons, almost seventy people, and well over two hundred horses and mules hit the trail for El Paso.

15

Twenty-two days after leaving Fort Clark, they pulled into the farm outside El Paso. Forewarned by a rider with a message, Pablo and the remaining hands who'd come south from Colorado were waiting to greet them. There were loud and boisterous reunions between Walt's men, and introductions for the *estancia* ranch hands and their families who'd come to join them.

After turning the horse herd into the corrals, to join those already waiting to make the journey north, the new arrivals were treated to a fiesta in miniature. Pablo had hired musicians from Paso del Norte across the river, who played for singing and dancing. The cook had prepared a mammoth meal with all the trimmings. By now everyone, including the Anglos and Navajos, had become accustomed to Mexican food. They ate until they bulged.

Eight-year-old Maria rapidly became a universal favorite, flitting among the groups, laughing and playing, and generally being thoroughly spoilt by everyone. "You're going to have trouble getting her to bed, Edelmira," Walt teased her mother.

"*Si, patrón,* but she has not enjoyed herself like this for years. It does my heart good to see her so happy."

"You look pretty happy, too," Walt observed, looking at

Sancho, who was holding Edelmira's arm very carefully, as if it would break.

"*Si, patrón.* Ah... I have a favor to ask, *patrón.* Edelmira has agreed to marry me." She blushed scarlet, and held even tighter to his arm. "We would like to ask the priest in Paso del Norte to perform the ceremony. Could I ask for my wages a little early, so I can pay for what will be needed?"

"Yes, of course, and I'll give you fifty dollars more. See me tomorrow morning to get the money. Go get everything fixed up, and we'll throw another party here as a wedding reception. When's the big day?"

"As soon as we can arrange it, *patrón* – we hope in two or three days."

The news traveled around the group like wildfire. There was an outburst of cheering, and people immediately began to plan the festivities. It soon became obvious that they wouldn't be leaving El Paso until the celebration was over. Grinning, Walt conceded the point.

"And so you should!" Colleen mock-scolded him. "It's going to be the biggest party they've ever seen. They'll remember their wedding for the rest of their lives!"

"Seems to me we ain't likely to forget yours, love. Your father's illness, an' the quick ceremony in his bedroom, then losin' him, then another wedding and a funeral, then dealin' with Sandoval... that was quite a time."

"It certainly was! We had more ups and downs to our wedding than I'd ever have imagined possible!"

Walt guffawed. "No, those came on our wedding night, when we finally got around to it."

She blushed, giggling. "Oh, *you! Men!*"

～

WALT TOOK the first opportunity to tell Pablo about the events surrounding Major d'Assaily's cache in Mexico, and how he'd recovered it, and all that had ensued. Pablo was particularly intrigued by the Ames knife. He fondled it lovingly, trying a few passes with it like the trained, skilled knife-fighter he was. "This was a good knife for its time, *señor,* but it could be made much better today," he mused.

"What do you mean?"

"It is like revolvers, *señor.* Remember the Walker Colt of 1846, and the Dragoon Colt of 1848? They were big and very heavy, more than four pounds. Metals were improved after that. The Army Colt of 1860 was made of silver steel. It weighed under three pounds, but was strong enough to fire the same size ball as the Dragoon. This Ames knife was made in 1849, you said?"

"Yes."

"Then it used earlier steels, like the Dragoon. It is very thick and heavy. More modern metals would allow it to be thinner and lighter, making it much handier. *Con su permiso, señor,* I would like to show this to the knifesmith here who made our throwing knives, that you ordered two years ago. I think he could copy its lines and make a much lighter, handier fighting knife."

"All right. Take it with you, and let me know what he says. Don't leave it with him, though. I want to return it to the Major's parents, if I can trace them."

Pablo returned the knife that evening. "The knifesmith has made drawings and taken measurements, *señor.* He will see about making a modern knife along the same lines. He says it will take several months. He will try different blade sizes, to get the right balance."

"What will it cost? I'll leave money with you."

Pablo made a gesture of negation. *"De nada, señor.* I will see to it. He will make one of them for me as well."

"Thank you. I'll look forward to getting it in due course. Tell the knifesmith that if he does a good job, and I like it, I may buy a dozen more of them. I've been looking for something to present to workers who do a real good job. A special knife might be just the thing."

As a wedding present for Edelmira and Sancho, Walt and Colleen bought a light buckboard from the local depot of the San Antonio to El Paso stage line. It had been languishing in the rear of the depot since breaking an axle, and had never been repaired. Fortunately, Fort Bliss had several spare wagon axles, one of which was just the right size. Money changed hands, and the axle was mounted on the wagon, which was rapidly repainted and overhauled. Walt had the hands install a raised platform in the back to serve as a bed, and five arched wagon bows. The ladies sewed a canvas cover to go over the bows, to provide protection from the weather and some privacy.

Grinning, the men urged Walt not to provide blocks for the buckboard's springs, but Colleen put her foot down. He had a local carpenter prepare four blocks, and showed Sancho how – and why – to use them. He also had the bedroom in the farm-house cleaned and prepared for the couple, and arranged for trustworthy sentries to keep interlopers away from it until after the wedding night. He knew what mischief his men could wreak, given half a chance.

The Navajo contingent looked after the horse herd while all the Mexican and Anglo hands crossed the river for the wedding. The churchgoers of Paso del Norte were amazed to see so many visitors in attendance. Even the priest remarked, during his sermon, on the presumed piety of his suddenly enlarged congregation. This reduced many of the hands to spluttering snorts and coughs, to mask their amusement. Colleen had to hide her face in her hands as her shoulders shook. None of the ranch hands fit that description, as Walt could have assured him.

At Colleen's urging, Walt spent another fifty dollars on food and drink for the reception. A sheep, a goat, a calf and a dozen chickens rotated on spits over coals, tables were loaded with side dishes and condiments, and barrels, bottles and jugs stood ready. The cook and her assistants came in for loud praise. The festivities continued for hours, with people eating, getting up to dance and talk, mingling with different groups, then going back for more food. Edelmira and Sancho were able to slip away in due course, aided and abetted by Walt and Pablo, who made sure they were left in peace and quiet for the evening. Maria was happy enough in her grandfather's care for one night. They slept in the newly converted buckboard for the first time, which was exciting enough for her that she didn't miss her mother at all.

THE FOLLOWING MORNING, while most of the revellers were still sleeping off their excesses, Pablo joined Walt and Colleen for breakfast. He clearly wanted to talk about something, but seemed hesitant. At last Walt took the bull by the horns. "Did you want to say something, *amigo?* You look like the cat's got your tongue."

Pablo half-smiled. *"Si, señor.* First, thank you for giving me my money right away. I would never have dreamed that two thousand dollars would grow so much in just four months!"

Walt nodded. He'd paid Pablo out of Major d'Assaily's gold, rather than make him wait to get back to Fort Union for his money. He'd done the same for Vicente. "Yes. This trip's been very profitable for all of us."

"Si, but now, I have been thinking. I put most of my savings into this, and they have multiplied. I want to have an *estancia,* a *rancho,* of my own one day. This money is a very good start towards that. It seems to me that if I stay here, and try to buy more horses for the Army, I could make more money."

Walt pursed his lips thoughtfully. "It depends how many they need. Remember, if they don't have any major campaigns, they don't wear out their horses, so they don't need to replace them. On the other hand, they'll always need at least five hundred or so every year in Texas and New Mexico, to replace natural wastage. If they fight the Indians, it might be several times that many, but how can you tell what's gonna happen? I knew I could sell a couple of thousand horses this year, because the Army told me so, and contracted with me for them. If I hadn't had that assurance before I left, I wouldn't have started out. I doubt I'll do this again."

"*Si, señor;* but if someone here in El Paso, closer to the Army's frontier forts, could listen carefully to what the soldiers are saying, he could have a better idea of what they need. He could then head into Mexico to buy the horses quickly, before someone further away could ride down here, or send riders, to do the same thing. If he moved fast, and knew where to find the horses in Mexico, he could get the Army all it needed within a month or two, before other sellers could provide them."

Walt began to smile. "Are you thinking of setting up in business for yourself?"

"If you don't mind, *señor,* yes. The officers at Fort Bliss know me now, and they trust me. Two or three years of hard work, and I might be able to save twenty thousand dollars, perhaps even more. That would be enough to buy the land I need, and I could bring breeding stock from Mexico, as you've done. I could have a small horse *rancho* of my own, perhaps two or three thousand acres."

"That's not so small," Colleen observed. "My father's *estancia* was only two and a half thousand acres, but he raised more than a hundred good horses a year on it, and sold them for enough money to support all of us."

"You'll need more than that," Walt warned. "Remember, you've not only got to buy the ranch, and build houses for you and your hands, and barns and stables for your horses. You've also got to buy your breeding stock. Then, it'll take a few years to breed enough to sell. All that time, you'll be paying expenses – wages, horse feed, more buildings and corrals, an' all that – but you won't earn an income from the ranch. You have to put aside enough to cover that, or plan to earn money some other way until the breeding program begins to make a profit."

Pablo nodded soberly. "I hear you, *señor*. You speak wisdom. I shall think on those things."

"Where will you live, to begin with?"

"If you will permit, *señor,* I would like to buy this farm from you. I'll use it as a base."

"No problem at all. You paid three hundred for it on my behalf when you got here, and I spent another hundred-odd on the new corrals and hay barns. You can have it for what it's cost me – four hundred dollars."

Pablo flushed. "Thank you, *señor*. I... I feel almost guilty about asking. You've treated me very well in the two years I've worked for you. I don't want to seem ungrateful by wishing to make a fresh start for myself."

"That's not ungrateful, Pablo. That's common sense. You'll never get rich on a monthly wage. You've got to strike out on your own to make big money. You've got a quick mind, and you work real hard. Given a mite o' luck, I reckon you'll succeed. To help, I'll tell Colonel Mackenzie and Fort Union you'll be available to get them horses in the future. They both know your name by now, so they'll be willing to use you again, I think."

"Thank you, *señor*."

Walt was struck by a sudden inspiration. "I'll do better than that. I'll grubstake you. Colonel Mackenzie expects trouble on the plains this year. If he's right, and a big campaign blows up, the Army's gonna need at least a thousand remounts by later in the year, perhaps more. Can't say for sure until we know how the fightin' goes. If it looks like that many will be needed, and if you can line up sellers in Mexico, I'll invest ten thousand dollars in your hoss buyin' late this year and early next year. I'll wire it to you through Wells Fargo. Added to your own money, that'll give you fifteen thousand or so to buy horses. Reckon up my ten thousand as a percentage of the total, and keep it in mind.

"If you do as well as we've done this year, you should be able to turn it into three times that much, maybe more, when you sell the hosses to the Army. Deduct ten thousand to pay me back, plus your expenses. What's left will be the profits. Take my percentage share of the profits, and divide it by two. You keep half, for doin' all the work, and I'll take half for providin' the money. You can wire it all back to me, again through Wells Fargo. You'll also have the full profits earned with your part o' the startin' money. Does that sound fair?"

Pablo's face shone. "Señor, that will be... it is *magnífico!* Thank you so much! I could never get a bank to lend me that much without security, which I do not have."

"Just use your head, and be careful about expenses. You've got to watch those like a hawk. They can get out of hand real easy."

"Where will you establish your *rancho?*" Colleen asked.

"I don't know yet, *señora.* I'm thinking of Colorado, after Señor Walt's example, but there is also New Mexico or Texas."

Walt said thoughtfully, "You should talk to Vicente. He and his *mesteñeros* are based in Las Cruces, two days' ride from here. Vicente told me last year that the days of old-style mustanging are almost over, because there are so few good wild horses left. He and his men will need a new way to make a living. Breaking and training horses on your *rancho* might suit them very well. If you can raise the money, they can provide the skills. It might be a good match."

Pablo's face lit up. "That's a very good idea, *señor!* I will talk to him today. Perhaps he and his men could ride into Mexico with me to buy horses. That would give me people I know I can trust."

Walt held out his hand. "The best of luck to you, Pablo. You've become, not just a hired hand or a gunman, but a friend. You'll always be welcome in my home, and I want you to keep in touch. I'll ship the rest of your belongings via Wells Fargo when I get home."

"Thank you, *señor*. It was a very good day for me when Isom asked if I was interested in working for you."

"Considering you saved me from Parsons' exploding cupboard, that was a very good day for me, too!"

FORT BLISS NEEDED to send a hundred horses up to Fort Stanton, and another hundred to Fort Union. Walt took advantage of the escort provided for them, and arranged to travel with the Army herd. They rolled out a week after arriving in El Paso, heading north. There were two more wagons on this leg of the journey; the newly married couple's buckboard, and another wagon bearing the cook Walt had hired at the farm, along with her family. She had asked to come to Colorado with him, to work on the ranch or in Pueblo. Given the excellent food she'd prepared for them, Walt was glad to hire her, and promised to find work for the rest of her family too.

The journey took them east of the Mescalero Apache reservation, along the western edge of the *Llano Estacado,* where grass was more plentiful than in the center of that desolate area. Colleen was fascinated by the flat terrain. "Why do they call it the 'Staked Plain'?" she asked.

Walt pointed. "See that stick there, just standing upright in the middle of nowhere?"

"Yes."

"That's prob'ly one of the stakes that first gave this place its name. See, it's so flat an' featureless, you can't tell where you are. There's no landmarks. It's easy to get lost and wander around until you run out o' food, or water, or both. In the old days, when people started crossing it, they'd plant stakes every so often, forming lines stretching for miles and miles, to show the way to the next waterhole or safe stopping place. The lines of stakes gave this place its name."

She laughed. "So it really was a 'staked' plain!"

"Yeah, but wind an' weather might blow over the stakes, or Indians might pull 'em up. If the line of stakes ran out, you had to remember which way they were goin' and keep to that course. That wasn't too hard if you had a compass, or could steer by the stars, but if you couldn't hold a course, you might find yourself in a world of hurt."

"I see. Is that why you line the tongue of our wagon on the North Star every night, before we go to bed?"

"It sure is. It's an old habit, dating back to the first pioneers to go west, and a real good one. Line up the tongue at night, and in the morning you know where north is. That makes it easier to set your course each day, even if you can't see a landmark."

Walt noticed that the Navajo scouts grew somber as the journey progressed. By the fifth day, their low spirits were so obvious that he took Nastas aside and asked about it.

"It is this place," the older man said sadly. "Many Navajo were forced to march here, on foot, in what we call the Long Walk, ten years ago. They went to Fort Sumner, and were forced to share the *Bosque Redondo* with the Mescalero Apache. Many of our people died here. We hear their spirits. They still call to us, asking us to remember them. The memories are bitter."

"I'm sorry." Walt reached out and gripped Nastas' arm in wordless sympathy. "At least your people were allowed to leave in due course."

"Yes, but only after four years. Many of our men were killed by Ute scouts and slavers. Many of our women and children were taken as slaves, and we have never heard of them again. The memories here set our teeth on edge."

"I wish I'd known more about this. I'd have traveled a different way, to spare you."

Nastas shook his head. "No, brother. This is the quickest way to Fort Union, so it is better for the horses. We shall take our memories of this place back to our reservation, and sing them to our brothers and sisters, so that we may all remember and honor our dead together. When we return to your ranch, we shall take our memories to Blanca Peak as well, to tell them to our ancestors."

They reached Fort Stanton on the eighth day, and delivered the first batch of horses. They rested there for just one day, then set out on the eleven-day leg to Fort Union.

Five days into the journey, the Navajo scouts warned that there were signs of an Indian presence; unshod horse tracks, a campfire, a dead deer that had been cut up for meat. Walt ordered everyone to be on higher alert than usual, and the Army patrol escorting the horses doubled their guard over the herd at night.

The following morning, at about the eleventh hour, Walt was riding his horse next to Colleen's when an Army outrider shouted an alert. Looking around, Walt saw a group of about fifteen Indians on a shallow rise, about half a mile away. Their horses stood motionless as the watched the horses and wagons move past.

Walt took out his spyglass and peered through it, then stiffened. "I'll be damned if that's not Laughing Raven! If it ain't him, it's his twin brother – and I think I recognize the rifle sleeve on his arm."

"He's the Kiowa you gave it to, back in Kansas?" his wife asked.

"The very same." Walt thought for a moment. "I'm gonna try to talk to him, see what's happening around here, and what may happen later this year."

"Walt! Be careful!"

"I will, honey. I ain't about to get in trouble. I'll handle this slow and easy."

He cantered over to the patrol commander, a sergeant, and explained what he wanted to do. The NCO obligingly halted the patrol, while Walt did the same to the horse herd and wagons. The sound of hooves slowed and ceased, and a cloud of dust raised by their passage slowly began to dissipate.

Walt began to walk his horse slowly towards the group of Indians. As he rode, he pulled his Winchester carbine from its saddle boot, levered a round into the chamber, and aimed it upward at a forty-five degree angle to the right. He pulled the trigger, and the flat *crack!* of the shot echoed across the plain. He opened the loading lever, then left it open as he reversed the rifle, holding it in his right hand by its muzzle. Raising it vertically above his head, with the open loading lever clearly visible, he kept riding slowly forward. When he was halfway between the wagons and the Indians, Walt halted his horse and returned the rifle to its boot; then he waited.

There was a brief, visible discussion among the Indians. Laughing Raven – if it was him – seemed to be arguing with those around him. Eventually he said something sharp, and cut his hand horizontally across his body, as if to shut down further debate; then he walked his horse slowly towards Walt. His rifle remained in the sleeve over his arm.

As the Indian grew nearer, Walt was more and more sure it was Laughing Raven; and the smile on the man's face showed that he recognized Walt in his turn. They came together, horses stopped only a few feet from each other.

Walt began speaking in the sign language known to all Plains Indian tribes. It was slow, because he had only one hand, but he used the hook on his left wrist to make motions approximating a hand sign when he could.

"It is good to see Laughing Raven once more. I hear you are a Dog Soldier now."

The Indian set the rifle sleeve across his saddle, and signed in his turn, "Yes. It is good to see you, too, Brings The Lightning. I have often thought about you. The medicine of my grandfather, which you gave to me, has done good things for me."

"I'm glad to hear it. Do those men follow you?"

"Yes, they follow me. We look for the herds of buffalo, that we may guide our people to them for the summer hunt."

"Have you found many?"

"Not yet." The Indian scowled. "We know many have been killed by the men with long rifles, who leave all their meat to rot and take only their hides and tongues. We shall surely kill any of them we meet. You are not hunting buffalo, are you?"

"No, we are not. I have been in Mexico, buying horses for my ranch. We are on our way home to Colorado."

"I remember you were on your way there when we first met, nine years ago. Have you made a home there for yourself and your wife, as you wished?"

"I have." Walt didn't bother to explain that his first wife had since died, and that he'd just remarried. He went on, "I am worried for you and your people. If there is a fight between you and the buffalo hunters, it may spark a bigger war that will engulf many people. Can there not be peace in this land?"

"Not so long as the men with long rifles cross into our territory to hunt. They are breaking your laws and ours when they do so. We shall stop them, no matter what."

Walt sighed. "If I were in your shoes, I should probably feel the same. However, I warn you as a friend: the bluecoats have just received many thousands of horses, and they are preparing. I do not want to see you hurt or killed."

Laughing Raven shrugged, a very European gesture, Walt thought. His fingers flew in a rapid succession of signs. "I must protect my people, and to do that, I must protect our hunting grounds. Without the buffalo, we are nothing. Their flesh feeds us, their hides shelter and clothe us. We cannot see them destroyed like this."

"I understand. I hope you will be safe, if it comes to that."

"I hope you will be safe too. I see your left hand is gone. Was that in war?"

"It was fighting bad men, outlaws. I lost my hand, but the man who took it lost his life."

"You did better than he, then." The Kiowa hesitated, then went on, "It will be best if you leave this place quickly. Many are gathering, Comanche, Kiowa and others. All are determined to stop the slaughter of the buffalo, and turn back the invasion of our land by white settlers. If we do not do so now, it will be too late. I would not like you, my friend, whom Satank also called friend, to be caught up in that."

"I thank you. I will be gone from here as soon as I can take my horses north."

Laughing Raven nodded. "They are good horses. I can see that even from this distance."

Walt smiled. "If you wait here, I shall show you."

Interest flickered on the Kiowa's face. "I shall wait."

Walt turned his horse, and cantered back to the herd. As he approached, he called, "Sam, catch me that big roan stallion, quick!" He pointed at it.

The former buffalo soldier uncoiled his lariat and made a quick hooley-ann throw to snare the stallion. The sixteen-hand horse was one of those Pablo's men had bought in Mexico, high-spirited and in excellent condition. Sam led it clear of the herd, while Walt fetched a hackamore from his wagon. He put the hackamore on the stallion, returned the lariat, then headed back towards Laughing Raven, leading the stallion behind him.

He drew up next to him, handed him the hackamore, then began signing again. "As a token of the friendship between us, please accept this horse. He will serve you well."

Laughing Raven's eyes glittered. The roan was larger than his horse, and better configured. It was a mount worthy of a chief. He hesitated, frowning. "I thank you, but I have no gift to give you in exchange."

"You have one gift in your power. If you remember, Satank gave my wife and I, and those traveling with us, the gift of free passage through the rest of the Kiowa hunting grounds in Kansas. You could do the same, and send word to your people to let us pass freely. We mean them, and you, no harm, after all."

The Kiowa's frown cleared. "That is true. I remember, and I shall give you the same gift. I shall pass the word to the rest of my people to let you go in peace. However, do not come back this way. My word will not protect you if the war clouds gather."

"I thank you. May the Great Spirit protect you and yours."

"And you."

In the Indian way, Laughing Raven did not say goodbye. He wheeled his horse and trotted back towards his men. The roan stallion whickered, but followed behind him without fighting the hackamore.

Walt watched him go, then cantered back to the herd. Colleen rode forward to join him, and Nastas and Vicente followed them to where the sergeant was waiting. Walt told them all what Laughing Raven had said. "Looks like there's gonna be fightin' for sure this summer," he finished somberly. "I'm glad we'll be outta here before the buffalo herds arrive. Once they do, the place is gonna be full of Indian hunting parties. It'll only take one spark to turn 'em into war parties overnight."

The sergeant spat expressively to one side. "Yeah, and with this patrol havin' only twenty men, we ain't strong enough to stop 'em ridin' right over us an' stealin' all our hosses. I'm glad that Injun said he'd pass the word to let us go. I'll ask you to tell the Commanding Officer at Fort Union what he said to you."

"I'll do that. Now, let's get going. The sooner we reach the fort, the happier I'll be!"

As the wagons and horses got under way again, Colleen asked, "Why did you give him one of your breeding stallions? That was a very good horse."

"It was, but keeping the peace with Laughing Raven and his

Kiowa was more important. By giving him just one horse, but a real good one, it was clear I was giving a gift to a friend, rather than paying some sort o' tribute to a more powerful enemy. He felt obliged to give me summat in exchange. That's what I was hopin' for, so I asked him in return to pass the word to let us go through in peace. He agreed. The last thing I want is to have a mess o' Kiowa or Comanche runnin' off with all our horses, not to mention what they might do to you."

She shivered. "Papa fought the Kickapoo and Lipan Apache in Mexico, and he's told me something of what they used to do to people they captured. If the gift of a horse helps keep us safe from that, it's worth it."

"I reckon so. Besides, I've got other stallions, includin' four I bought from your father. They're even better than the one I gave away."

She frowned, puzzled. "Four? You bought five of them."

"Yeah, but Nastas will get one. He's more than earned it."

16

Major Price, commanding officer of the 8th Cavalry detachment at Fort Union, greeted Walt, and listened attentively to his report on his encounter with Laughing Raven. When Walt had finished, he grunted expressively, and moved across to a big map on the wall of his office. Walt followed him.

"They're coming south and west out of the Indian Territory," he said, tracing their direction of travel from the reservation near Fort Sill, four hundred and fifty miles away. "My scouts have already reported at least ten bands of Comanche and Kiowa. Your Laughing Raven's the eleventh. You say he warned you they'll paint for war if the buffalo hunters cross the boundary into their lands?"

"He was real firm 'bout that, sir. They won't stand for any more of it."

"Then it'll be war," the officer said flatly. "We simply can't stop every skin-hunter. More of them than ever are headed this way, because they've shot out the herds further north. There's too much money to be made from buffalo hides. They'll keep coming, and they'll cross the line, and next thing you know we'll be hip-deep in angry Indians."

Walt sighed, but said nothing.

"We're going to need all those fine horses you brought us from Mexico," the officer went on, turning back to his desk. "We'll at least be well mounted if it comes to a fight. It's likely to be long-drawn-out and cover a wide area, so we'll go through remounts real fast. You might be able to sell us a couple thousand more by this time next year."

"In that case, Major, I suggest you write or wire to Pablo Gomez in El Paso. He brought in many of ours, and he's staying on there to get more as you need them."

Major Price wrote Pablo's name and address in his daybook. "I'll keep that in mind, and pass the word to our horse buyers. I think we'll have business for him, come the fall. Now, let's deal with your bank drafts." He frowned. "Do you know how much trouble you put us to, by insisting on payment in gold when you returned here? Couldn't you have simply deposited the government drafts in your bank account?"

Walt shook his head. "I realize it was a lot of work for you, sir, but look at it from my side. My bank tells me it'll take three to six months for the U.S. government to pay those drafts. Until that happens, they won't credit the funds to my account. I've got businesses to run. I can't afford to wait that long to have money to spend."

The Major's attitude softened. "I didn't know it took that long. I suppose you had to do it this way, then – but it was a lot of extra work for us. We had to apply for the gold six months in advance. It took a special escort to bring it from Washington D.C. all the way out here, plus a second special shipment a few weeks ago, after Colonel Mackenzie asked General Sheridan to authorize more money for remounts."

Walt grinned. "If it took the Department of War six months to get the gold to you, I guess that explains why my bank couldn't get it any faster."

Major Price shook his head ruefully. "I can hardly argue with that!"

Walt handed over the bank drafts, in exchange for almost $60,000 in double-eagle twenty-dollar gold coins. They weighed in at over two hundred pounds, so he had to get several Army NCO's to help him carry the leather satchels back to his wagon. Colleen made space for them between her trunks, and he stacked them carefully out of sight.

"Best be careful," a sergeant warned him as he handed over his satchel. "If folks find out what this is, you'll have every thief, road agent and grifter in the Territory after you."

"That's why we're armed, and I've made sure my men know how to use their guns."

The sergeant looked around, and a smile came to his face. "You've sure got enough of them. I reckon you c'n make a mighty good case for keepin' the money, iffen you have to."

"Yeah. After all, I paid a lot o' money for all this breeding stock. The horses are gold on the hoof. Compared to them, looking after gold in a wagon is pretty easy!"

THEY STAYED at Fort Union for three days, to rest the horses and prepare for the last stretch to Walt's ranch in the Wet Mountain Valley. Those who'd left there with him in November had by now covered between one-and-a-half and two-and-a-half thousand miles, depending on where in Mexico they'd been sent. They'd been on horseback for between eighty and a hundred and forty days, and were very tired of life on the trail. They longingly expressed their desire to get home, and stay there for a while. The *estancia* workers had traveled less far, many in wagons rather than on horseback, but were no less eager to settle down.

Walt decided to take a westerly route via Taos and Fort Garland, keeping as far away from the Texas Panhandle and

Indian hunting grounds as he could. It would add an extra day or two's travel, but the greater safety afforded by distance from the disputed area would be worth it. Nastas looked at the map as he traced out the route, and nodded his approval.

"If you will allow," he said in Spanish, so that his men could understand as they gathered around, "I would like to leave you at Taos and head west to our home. It will shorten our journey. We can deliver our horses, see our families, and rest for a week or two. Some of my men will want to stay there, but others will come back to your ranch with me, and more will join us. We can be with you by the middle of June. Will that be soon enough for the Army, do you think?"

"I hope so. I don't know whether or when they'll send me a message, but I can't think it'll be too quickly. They won't mobilize for action until there's been some incident that warrants it. I'd say July or August is more likely."

"Then we shall spend more time with our families, and join you by the end of June. We shall visit Blanca Peak, and help you with your horses, and learn from the workers you brought from Mexico. The *estancia*'s herd is proof they know more than any of us about how to breed and raise the Spanish line."

"I agree. When we reach Taos, all of you can choose your horses. Each scout has four horses comin', and the herd boys two apiece. You've got ten mares and a stallion coming from the *estancia*'s herd as well, plus seventy-two horses to pay for the breeding stock you brought me, and your group leader's pay an' bonus, too. I'll give you another five hundred dollars to help with food and travel expenses goin' home, an' comin' back to Colorado. Oh – and I'll give you that Winchester 1873 carbine for Isom. I had the woodworker in El Paso make another deeper fore-end when he made one for my carbine. All Isom will have to do is transfer the ring for his hook from his old 1866 model to the new one. I'm also gonna give you the last one of those good red blankets we took from the

Comancheros. It's for the new baby. Doli can cut it up and sew it to the right size."

Nastas beamed with pleasure. "I thank you, for myself, and my men, and for Isom and Doli. You are very generous. I wish all white men were as you are."

"No, you don't. You'd get so tired of so many people like me, you'd scalp us all!"

That evening, he told Colleen of the arrangements. She entirely approved. "They're good people. How did you persuade them to come and work on your ranch for a while, and come to Mexico with you?"

"They get restless and frustrated on the reservation. Isom solved that for Nastas' family when he married his daughter, and brought all of them to live on his spread; but there are plenty more who don't have that outlet. Nastas was real grateful that we rescued his daughter. He promised to sell me breeding stock. When the time came, he asked if he could bring some other Navajo with him, to let them learn about raising horses on my ranch. I said sure, and invited him to bring them to Mexico too. I offered to pay them in horses. They jumped at the chance. O' course, the fact they might end up in a fight or two didn't hurt none. They're still warriors at heart, after all."

"So Nastas gained status as a warrior through fighting those *bandidos* with you?"

"Yes, and all the Navajo did from the fight against the *Comancheros*. If we scout for the Army later this year, they'll gain even more. Nastas'll have no trouble getting his pick of the other Navajo to come with him."

"Scout for the Army? And you said 'we'? How are you involved?" Colleen's voice was suddenly dubious.

"Uh... this was agreed before I met you, love. Sorry – I plumb forgot to tell you. Colonel Mackenzie is thinkin' o' using Navajo scouts if he takes the field later this year. He asked me to go along with 'em as a sort o' chief scout, to help 'em understand what the Army wants."

"Won't that be dangerous?"

Walt shook his head. "I don't think so. We ain't gonna be takin' part in any charges. Scouts find where the enemy's at and tell the main body, then sit back an' watch while they do the work. I don't reckon it'll be all that risky."

"Well... I hope you're right. I can't say I'm happy, but if you promised Colonel Mackenzie before you met me, there's not much to be done. Just be careful!"

"I will, honey. I've got you to live for now."

"All right. Now, there's something else I've been wondering about. What's your house like, on the ranch?"

Walt shook his head. "I don't have one. I built small apartments for Nate, my ranch manager, and myself in the administration building. I reckoned I'd wait to build a proper house until I had a wife who could help design it the way she wanted it."

Colleen dimpled. "That was sweet of you! We'll do that together – but where will we live in the meantime? Not in the wagon, I hope? And what about in Pueblo?"

Walt shook his head. "I have another apartment there, in the administration building of the transport company. It'll be too small for both of us. We'll rent or build a house there, too. I already have a site. Rose and I bought it together, but she died before we could build."

He sent two telegraph messages the following morning. One was to Nate at the ranch, asking him to prepare whatever accommodation was available for the *estancia* workers, and begin planning where to build their new homes. The other was to Samson Moses, manager of the freight yard in Pueblo, asking him to send a good-quality double bed out to the ranch as quickly as possible. His wife should choose and ship good-quality bedding, dressers, and other basic furniture a couple would need. He was also to reserve a room for them at a good hotel near the freight yard, and another two rooms for Guillermo, Sancho, Edelmira and Maria. Walt would pay for the family's accommodation while they looked for a house, which he'd buy for them.

"We'll have an architect draw up plans for both our homes, in town and at the ranch," he promised Colleen. "No cheap shacks for us!"

"How will you get the materials out to the ranch, and all the fittings and fixtures?"

"Well, I know a man who owns a transport outfit. I reckon I can persuade him to help us."

She giggled. "I know what! I'll bribe him to help us, by sleeping with him."

He opened his eyes wide in mock horror. "You wouldn't!"

"You bet I would, buster!"

He laughed aloud as he hugged her. "Thank you for helping me to laugh again. It's been a long while since I had this much fun with anyone."

Walt sent a third telegraph message before they left, to the Pinkerton Detective Agency's office in Pueblo. He gave the agency all the information he had about the late Major d'Assaily's parents, and asked them to trace his family. They were to send their report to him at Ames Transport. He was not looking forward to telling the family how their son and brother had died, but the Major's long silence must surely have been enough for them to guess that he had not survived. At least Walt would be able to return his belongings to them, and tell them how he had died, and allow them to bury him and mourn him properly.

THEY ROLLED out for Taos the following day, heading northwest. They took seven days to cover the distance, slowed by the trail's passage through mountains and valleys. The wagons labored up and down the slopes, and the horse herd had to be held back to stay with them.

When they got to Taos, Walt halted the drive a couple of miles outside town. He sent a wagon into town to buy supplies for the final leg, then allowed the Navajo scouts and herd boys to choose their own horses, as he'd promised them the previous year. They could take their pick of the animals brought back from Mexico, except for those from the *estancia*. They lingered over their selection, weighing up options, and in some cases swapping a horse they'd already chosen for one picked by another.

While they did that, Nastas chose seventy-two of the Mexican horses in payment for the breeding stock he'd delivered to Walt last year. That done, he made his selection of ten mares and a stallion from the *estancia*'s stock. He didn't waste time over it, having had many weeks with the animals during which to study them and make his choice. The other Navajo looked on enviously as he drove them to join the others they would be taking home.

"He's picked the cream of our horses," Colleen said softly as they watched.

"He has, but he's earned them," Walt assured her. "Without his backing, I'd never have come to your ranch, and we'd never have met."

"In that case, he's welcome to them!"

"Yes. It's not like those he didn't choose are bad horses, either. They're just about as good as his. I'm more than satisfied with them."

Walt wrote out a bill of sale for all the horses, then paid the Navajo the balance of what was owed them, plus Nastas' wages and the five hundred dollars in travel money he'd promised them. They loaded their pack saddles with food for the ten-day journey to their home on Isom's spread, and mounted their horses. With loud calls of farewell, and promises to return, they bunched their herd and set out westward.

Sam Davis lingered for a moment. "It's been real good to ride with you again, boss. I reckon Isom's just about got things runnin' as he wants them now. We've taught the Navajo what they need to know about range ridin', cattle herdin' and suchlike, an' they've taught us a lot more'n we knew before about horses. I reckon Isom won't need me much longer. When the time comes, d'you reckon you might have work for me again?"

"Anytime you want, Sam. D'you want to work on the ranch, or in the transport business, like you did before?"

"I'd kinda like to get back on the wagons, boss. I've had my fill for awhile o' chasin' cows an' horses around."

Walt laughed. "Show up at the transport yard in Pueblo, and Samson will sign you up. I'll tell him you'll be along sometime. He'll be glad to see you. You won't be a teamster for long, though. I reckon you've learned enough since you first joined us, and all you've done since then, that you're almost ready to be a wagon-master an' lead your own train. That pays better, too." He hesitated as a thought struck him. "In fact, if you come back with Nastas in a few weeks, I may have a scouting job with the Army for you. I'd agreed to be the civilian chief scout for the Navajos with Colonel Mackenzie, but if you're here, I can send you instead. You were a buffalo soldier and a corporal, so you can do that job as well as I can. That way, I can concentrate on buildin' up the ranch, an' seein' to Ames Transport after bein' away for so long."

"I'll see what Isom says. If he can spare me that soon, I'll be there. Thanks, boss."

Sam doffed his hat to Colleen, then turned his horse and galloped after the Navajo.

Colleen turned to Walt and hugged him. "Thank you for thinking of that, darling! If you don't have to go with the scouts, I must admit, I'll sleep easier at night." She dimpled. "Warmer, too, with you there."

Walt winked at her. "Figured you might. Let's see what we can fix up."

As they left Taos behind them, Colleen noticed that Walt was becoming silent, more withdrawn than usual. She left it until mid-afternoon, then tackled him gently.

"Honey, you've been kinda quiet all day. You look like something's eating you. What's wrong?"

He sighed. "It's... well, I can show you better than tell you. Let me get a horse saddled for you, and we'll take a short ride together."

Consumed with curiosity, she waited in her buggy until the horse was ready, then swung lithely into the saddle. By now the hands were used to her divided skirts, and no-one turned a hair to see her riding astride. Any experienced horseman knew that a rider had far better control over their mount that way. For the wife of a horse rancher to do so, rather than ride side-saddle in a typically ladylike fashion, made good sense to the hands.

Walt said as much as they rode off together to the eastward of the trail. "I reckon they're gettin' used to you ridin' astride."

"Just wait until I start wearing men's trousers. That'll shake them!"

He stared incredulously. "You ain't serious, are you?"

"Why not? When we're out on the ranch, and I ride with you or have work to do somewhere, is there anything more practical?"

"No, and I can't say I'll mind the view, but for most of the men it's gonna be a real scandal, you mark my words!"

"Oh, well. I'll start slowly. I'll wear a thin dress over the trousers, so they don't reveal too much. Now, what are you going to show me?"

"It's not far; just at the top of this next rise, in fact." They halted their horses, and he pointed. "You see that farmhouse over there, with a barn across the yard and half a dozen workers' cottages beyond it?" He handed her a pair of binoculars.

"Yes, I see it." She adjusted the binoculars and studied the buildings.

"That's where Parsons ended up – the man who caused the death of my first wife. He ran for it after she died, 'cause he knew I'd come after him once I recovered. I traced him to this place after months of searchin', and hired a few gunhands to back my play. We hit the house at dawn one morning in late January. He had three gunmen with him. We killed 'em, although we lost two of our own doin' that. Parsons ran for it, got to the barn, grabbed a hoss and headed for Taos, back that way. I shot his hoss before he could get too far, then killed him, over there." He pointed to a slight rise in the ground on the far side of the farmhouse, about a mile from where their horses stood.

She looked through the binoculars. "There's a big animal's skeleton still there, just below the rise."

Walt fished out his spyglass and looked for himself. "Well, I'll be darned. So there is! The farm workers must've decided it was too much like hard work to move or bury the horse." He scanned lower. "There's four graves behind the house now. They weren't there when I was last here. I reckon that's where they buried Parsons and his men."

Colleen lowered the binoculars and looked at him soberly. "Did it help you, to avenge Rose like that? Did it make you feel better?"

"It wasn't revenge, love. I knew all along that killin' Parsons wouldn't bring her back. Rather, I was dead set on makin' sure he'd never do that to another woman, or hurt another man the way her death hurt me. He was bad clear through. He'd made a fortune stealin' from other people before he tried to steal from me. I dealt with his men that time, but that led to everythin' that followed. He *had* to be stopped. I wasn't burnin' up with anger or hatred. It just needed doin', and I had the best reason in the world to do it. Afterwards... well, afterwards I just felt kinda empty."

She reached over and squeezed his arm. "I don't understand exactly what you were feeling, of course, but I'm glad you didn't take pleasure in his death. I hope I'd feel that way, if I were in your shoes."

He grinned at her. "Wouldn't fit. My boots are like buckets compared to yours!"

She laughed. "Come on. Let's get back to the others. After supper, I reckon I know just how to take your mind off Parsons!"

"You're beautiful enough to take my mind off anyone an' everything, anytime you want to."

She dimpled. "Really? I'll have to experiment, later on tonight."

"You're on!"

17

Their arrival at the Rafter A ranch was greeted with a sigh of relief by all those who'd ridden so far for so long, and an explosion of pent-up joy from the families who'd waited just as long for their menfolk to return. The ranch hands who weren't yet married were given powerful reasons to consider that option as they watched the ecstatic reunions between husbands and wives, fathers and children.

Walt took Colleen to meet Nate. "This is my manager. He's been workin' darn hard over the winter. There's gotta be twice as many buildings as there were when we left."

"Honored to meet you, ma'am," Nate greeted Colleen, then looked back at Walt. "Soon as I got your telegraph message from Eagle Pass about bringin' all the *estancia* hands back with you, I got hold of Samson. He ordered a bunch o' planks an' such, and sent out a wagon train with them and everything else we needed, along with a dozen workmen. I had 'em put up those two long bunkhouses over there. They're divided into little apartments, each with a front room an' one or two bedrooms. There's outhouses out back, an' I built a separate bathhouse, with different sides for men an' women. You told me you was married, too, so I took in two of the guest rooms an' added them to your apartment. I turned one of 'em into a small bathhouse, so you an' your wife can have some privacy. I'll use the main one with the hands."

"That's wonderful!" Colleen enthused. "Thank you so much for thinking of all that! The families can settle down right away."

"Yes, ma'am. Over the next few months we'll build separate cottages for those who want them. I reckon, bein' Mexican, they'll probably prefer adobe over wood, but the boss can decide what he wants to use later."

"I don't mind adobe," Walt told him. "It's pretty fireproof, too, which may be useful someday. We'll build ourselves a house out here, but that'll be of stone or brick."

"Figured as much. So, d'you reckon all those months and all those miles were worth it?"

Walt hugged Colleen. "I've come back with a new wife, which is the best and most important part of the trip for me. I've brought back almost eighty thousand dollars in gold, and more'n sixty of the best breeding stock I've ever seen, from the *estancia*. There's well over two hundred more darned good horses from Mexico, and a dozen six-mule wagons I bought to bring our new workers here. Can you think of any way this could have worked out better?"

Nate shook his head, laughing. "When you put it like that, no, boss, I sure can't – unless your wife has a sister?" He looked hopefully at Colleen.

She laughed. "No sister, I'm afraid; but Walt's friend Pablo stayed in El Paso, to buy more horses for the Army later in the year. If you want to ride into Mexico with him, you never know. Lightning might strike twice in the same country."

Nate shook his head vigorously. "Not me, ma'am! I was just jokin'. I'm a confirmed bachelor."

Walt rolled his eyes. "You shouldn't have said that. Now you're bound to meet the right woman in no time at all, just so the good Lord can show you who's boss and make you eat your words!"

WALT AND COLLEEN stayed at the ranch for a week, helping the new arrivals settle down, watching Nate integrate the new stock into the existing herd and breeding program, and relaxing after so long a journey. Colleen thoroughly approved of the new private bathhouse Nate had built for them, complete with its own wood-fired water heater. "That was so *thoughtful* of him!" she exclaimed after she'd tried it. "Why papa never thought to add one to the *estancia,* I don't know. We always heated water in cauldrons for our baths. After so much washing in cold water on the trail, I reckon I might get addicted to this real fast."

"We'll build a proper boiler and bathhouse into our new homes, here and in Pueblo," Walt promised her.

During long conversations with Walt and Nate, Colleen asked many questions about the breeding program they were setting up. Nate explained, "We can't make money sellin' cheap horses. Everyone an' his brother's doin' that already. We want to breed quality hosses, ones people will pay more to own. Walt an' I sat down and figured out two ways to approach it.

"The first is wagon teams. Normal hosses are a mite too light for that job in mountain country like Colorado. They don't have the stamina for all those hills, 'specially in a cold winter. Draft horses do, but they eat three times as much, an' need a lot of water, too. On the trail, that can cut into the amount of freight the wagons can carry. Walt wants to see about cross-breeding American Morgans with French Percherons, to get a lighter horse than a draft breed, but heavier and stronger than a standard breed, one that won't need so much food and water but can haul better in the mountains. We reckon it'll take five to ten years to get that right. Walt'll be goin' east to buy some Morgan an' Percheron breedin' stock next year."

Walt noted, "We'll test the cross-breeds on our freight wagons, so we can make sure they do what we need. I reckon we'll save a bundle breedin' our own, rather than payin' someone else to do that; and if they're successful, we'll make another bundle selling 'em."

Nate nodded. "The second is the Spanish strain of ridin' horses, like those the Navajo breed, and on your *estancia*. They're just too good-lookin' for words, and they run like the wind. People who want a showy horse will love 'em, and we expect there'll be a big demand for them for horse-racin', too."

Colleen grimaced. "Not like Mexican horse races, I hope, where they run them to death in a single season!"

"Not at all, ma'am. A man can make good money betting on hosses in the mining camps an' the cities. It makes 'em an investment, so he'll pay to look after them. We'll aim further afield, too, maybe even as far as the coasts. The transcontinental railroad makes that possible. If we breed a few real good racehorses, an' they make a name for themselves, people will be comin' to us to buy their brothers an' sisters. We can breed 'em a lot faster than developin' a new, mixed breed o' wagon horse, so this place can make a profit a lot sooner."

"I suppose you're right."

Walt added, "We might look at cutting horses, too – the special cow ponies that are bred to work in close with the cattle, to cut 'em out from the herd or separate cows from their calves for brandin'. I talked with Tyler Reese about it. Texas cowhands are real fond of a good cutting horse, but they reckon they have to be born with that attitude. They say, if the hoss has the gift, he can be trained, but you can't teach a hoss without it how to do it. I don't know about that, but I reckon if we can breed a couple of real good cutting horses to some high-quality mares, we might get a better strain of cutting horse out of it. It's worth a try. Tyler's promised to keep his eyes open for some real good cuttin' horses. He'll buy 'em and send 'em to me."

THAT EVENING, after enjoying the comforts of their new bathhouse once more and sharing supper with the hands in the communal cookhouse and dining hall, Walt and Colleen took a walk in the moonlight. The early summer air was pleasantly warm, and the air was redolent with the scent of mountain air, trees, and the last of the spring flowers.

"That's quite an ambitious breeding program Nate outlined today," she said thoughtfully as they strolled.

"I guess it is. It won't happen overnight, o' course. We've got a long way to go."

"Yes, we have. As it happens, there's another breeding program for you to think about, darling – one that's going to happen a lot faster than that."

"Oh, yeah? What is it?"

She stopped, turned to face him, and grinned as she looked up at him. "Darling, you can be very dense sometimes. I'm going to have a baby!"

For a moment Walt was too thunderstruck to say a word. He gaped at her in astonishment. At last he managed to stammer, "I – I'm gonna be a *father?*"

"You sure are, honey. You've been playing the stallion to my mare ever since we got married, remember?"

He felt as if champagne were bubbling in his veins. "A *baby*... well, I'll be damned!"

She frowned slightly. "Why are you so surprised? It was bound to happen, the way you and I enjoy each other so often."

"Oh, sure, but... you see, Rose was bad hurt in a buggy accident before we met. She couldn't have children. She told me that before we married, and I guess I grew to accept I'd never be a father. Meetin' you kinda drove everything else outta my mind. I never gave kids a second thought!"

"Well, you'd better, buster! We've got one coming, and I don't aim to stop at just one. You're too good a man not to have a lot more of you runnin' around the place."

He knew he was grinning foolishly, but he didn't care. "I can say the same about you. You're too good a woman not to have more of you, too."

"Then we'd better get on with building our houses, dear. The baby's going to need a roof over his head, or hers."

"We'll head for Pueblo in the mornin', and hire an architect, an' start planning right away." He hesitated. "Ah... does this mean I shouldn't be... er... botherin' you any more?"

She burst out laughing. "Silly! The baby won't be here for seven months or so yet, and I'm a normal, healthy, red-blooded woman. You're not getting away with that excuse!"

He grinned. "No excuse, love, just a man who ain't real sure what he's just got himself into."

"You'll find out soon enough. Now, walk me back to the apartment, so you and I can get into it again!"

AUTHOR'S NOTE

The tension between Indian tribes – the Comanche and Kiowa in particular – and buffalo hunters, would-be ranchers and settlers in the Texas Panhandle and surrounding regions grew steadily worse with the westward expansion of white settlement after the Civil War. The buffalo hunters brought matters to a head after they'd thinned out the central herds so much that hunts there were no longer as profitable as they'd been. They wanted to shift their operations to the abundant herds of buffalo in the southern part of the USA.

Hundreds of thousands of the creatures grazed on Indian land in what is today central and western Oklahoma, and on traditional Indian hunting grounds in the Panhandle and surrounding plains areas of Texas. The tribes weren't about to tolerate commercial hunting there. Buffalo formed their staple diet, and provided furs, hides and many other requirements. They knew that if the buffalo died, their entire way of life would die with them; and they were determined to prevent that at any cost – even war, if necessary. The US Army, on the other hand, regarded the extermination of the buffalo as an essential part of defeating the tribes. It would force them onto reservations where they could be controlled.

Attempts were made to regulate the situation, leading to the Medicine Lodge treaty of 1867; but such agreements were increasingly honored more in the breach than in the observance. Clashes between buffalo hunters, settlers, and cattlemen on the one hand, and Comanche and Kiowa on the other, grew more and more frequent – and bloody – during the early 1870's. They led to the Red River War, which broke out in June 1874 with what became known as the Second Battle of Adobe Walls. It was during that fight that scout Billy Dixon made his world-famous shot with a Sharps buffalo rifle, hitting a Comanche brave at a later-surveyed range of 1,538 yards (almost nine-tenths of a mile). The war ended in 1875 with the defeat of the Indian tribes, and their confinement to reservations in the Indian Nations (today part of central and eastern Oklahoma).

The US Army began preparing for hostilities by sending more soldiers to the chain of frontier forts it had erected in Texas and New Mexico. Military leaders recognized that infantry could not move fast enough on foot to catch up with Indian raiders on horseback, so they increased the proportion of mounted troops among their forces. That, in turn, led to a demand for more horses. The need, as described in the early pages of this book, was very great. Several people sought new ways to provide what the Army wanted, and was willing to pay for. Walt Ames' horse-buying forays into Mexico are thus based on actual events.

The character of Don Thomas O'Halloran is also based on fact. Many Irish emigrated to Mexico in the first half of the 19th century, and fought for that country in the Mexican-American War from 1846-1848. Other Irish immigrants deserted from US forces to form Saint Patrick's Battalion on the Mexican side. Don Thomas' description of what happened to them is accurate. The 1999 film *One Man's Hero,* starring Tom Berenger, depicts the history of the *Batallón de San Patricio,* and has received praise from critics. The unit is remembered at annual ceremonies in Mexico and Ireland to this day.

Walt's adventures will continue as he's drawn into the Red River War and events surrounding it, and tries to track down Major Gilbert d'Assaily's surviving relatives.

PETER GRANT
Texas, August 2019

ABOUT THE AUTHOR

Peter Grant was born and raised in Cape Town, South Africa. Between military service, the IT industry and humanitarian involvement, he traveled throughout sub-Saharan Africa before being ordained as a pastor. He later immigrated to the USA, where he worked as a pastor and prison chaplain until an injury forced his retirement. He is now a full-time writer, and married to a pilot from Alaska. They currently live in Texas.

See all of Peter's books at his Amazon.com author page, or visit him at his blog, Bayou Renaissance Man, where you can also sign up for his mailing list.

BOOKS BY PETER GRANT

SCIENCE FICTION:

FANTASY:

WESTERNS:

The Ames Archives

Brings The Lightning

Rocky Mountain Retribution

Gold On The Hoof

A River Of Horns

Silver In The Stones *(forthcoming)*

ANTHOLOGIES:

Forged In Blood (ed. Michael Z. Williamson)

Terra Nova: The Wars of Liberation (ed. Tom Kratman)

Trouble in the Wind (ed. Chris Kennedy and James Young)

Tales Around The Supper Table (ed. J. L. Curtis)

MEMOIR:

Walls, Wire, Bars And Souls

Printed in Great Britain
by Amazon

20836544R00130